HUNTER

A NOVEL BY

VAL GALE

ISBN #: 979-8-218-96583-9

Published by Val Gale Trans Books

Editor: Carol Burbank —cburbank@storyweaving.com

Cover Design: Rachel Denis — freshmen.co@gmail.com

Book Design: Patrise Henkel — www.patrise.com

DEDICATION

To all the misfits and tortured souls,

I see you.

Without your voice

this would not be possible.

May you find recognition and comfort in my pages.

CHAPTER 1

The world was distorted and blurry when Hunter finally unsealed his eyes. The medicine pumping in his veins beat in unison with his heart. He tried to move but was enclosed within a cocoon.

Where am I? Hunter spoke through his cracked and dry lips. It was so hot.

Finally, he managed to push the blanket and sheets aside, and pulled up his hospital robe. He ran his fingers across the train tracks of mostly healed scars on his torso, lingering on his fuzzy, but thickening chest hair. He knew the scars were still shiny, even though it had been a few years. The doctors had told him they would take a couple years to fade.

His sweat smelled strong and good. Despite his nausea, Hunter voiced weakly. I'm all right.

He reached down lower to check out his bandages. "Shit! Is this blood?" The IV in his hand tugged when he tried to yank them away, but they were soaking wet. Hunter struggled to sit up despite the pain.

Suddenly the door flew open, and a white uniform rushed toward him. "Stop! You will pull the needles out. Lean back! Here you go…" The nurse adjusted his pillow.

"Sorry, I thought they were… Could I have a drink of water? It's so hot!" Hunter wiped his forehead with his drenched gown.

"Of course. Narcotics raise your body temperature." The nurse filled a cup with water and big chunks of ice. In her other hand was a cloth.

"Ohhh, that's superb, Hunter sighed while she dabbed the damp fabric across his sweaty forehead. She found her way to Hunter's chiseled chest and slowly ran the cool cloth the length of his bumpy scars.

"These scars are healing nicely. Still recent though. How long ago?" she asked, continuing her task.

"Three years ago. You're observant. Most medical people just pretended they don't exist."

"These procedures take a lot of time and commitment." She wrung out the cloth and examined the bandages.

"Don't forget money," Hunter added.

She grinned and nodded. "I need to change your dressing. I will be back."

As she walked away her neat blonde ponytail bounced with every step. Her natural curves filled the nurse's uniform in all the right places.

"She's beautiful." Hunter exhaled out loud. The door swung gently shut.

Sleepily, he thought about his mother, once as beautiful as that nurse. Vanity is a psychological mind fuck. She warned Hunter once – beauty just brought women grief. Men promised her everything only to abandon her when her movie star looks began to fade. Finally, she settled for his father. She was still beautiful though, in those early days. His father's love affair with the bottle and his jealousy enraged him. Even so, she always dressed like a movie star.

Hunter's vanity was different than his mother's. His was for survival. He brushed his fingers across the bandage. Still wet. And it was starting to really hurt.

"Here we are. Let's get you cleaned up." The enchanting nurse had returned.

Her manicured nails worked diligently and gently to shift the bandage. Hunter watched her, drawn to her high cheekbones and ivory skin. She had inviting, ocean blue eyes. Not even a blemish on her face. She probably came from German stock.

"How does it look down there? I'm sore." Hunter grimaced as she removed the old bandages away.

"I brought you some pain medicine. There's no infection, and the tissue is the right color. There's a little bleeding, so try not to move around too much. All set, Hunter." She drew his sheet up carefully.

"You know my name, but I don't know yours."

"It's Cate. Here – take both pills."

She was a little shaky handing him the pill cup, and it slipped from her hands.

"I am so sorry!" Cate exclaimed. "I dropped them on the floor. I'll get you some new ones."

She scurried out of the room and went to the dispensary, putting in a new order. "I need to be careful," Cate mumbled as she placed the two dirty pills in her pocket and retrieved two clean ones for Hunter.

Her shoes squeaked in the hallway and into his room. "Here you go — I freshened up your water too. These will help with the pain. Get some rest - I will check on you later."

"Thank you, Cate." After she left, her fragrance lingered in the air. Hunter took his pills and began to relax, listening to the rhythm of beeping monitors that slowly rocked him to sleep, and dreams.

"No! this can't be happening!" Lisa screamed as she jerked her hand back from her soiled underwear. "Blood! How can this happen! I'm a boy not a girl!" Lisa jumped into the shower to cleanse her body from the unwanted intrusion. She avoided soaping her chest - puberty was already betraying her. In the steamy mirror, Lisa pushed her breasts flat and admired the effect.

"How handsome I would be with a goatee and sideburns."

Lisa began her daily routine then, binding her chest and carefully placing a wadded-up sock down her boxer briefs.

"Always to the left." Lisa reminded herself. Today was visiting day with her father, and she wanted to look presentable. Levis, a white T-shirt with the sleeves rolled up. A black comb in her back pocket to keep her hair slicked back in a duck tail like the Fonz. The buckles on her motorcycle boots chimed together wherever she walked, a grand entrance. Lisa was saving up for a leather jacket to complete the result.

They were going to his company picnic at the fairgrounds. Lisa loved to ride the amusement park rides. They made her invincible. Her stomach would drop with the same sensation she would get when Sara looked at her.

"Lisa, your dad is here!" Her mom's voice hollered down the stairs.

She went out the back door without saying goodbye. Today was her day. Her mom would spoil it by rolling her eyes at her "outfit."

"Lisa, hey, how are you?" Her dad had combed his salt and pepper hair back as usual to cover up an expanding bald spot. He rolled his cigarettes up in his sleeve and wore his wallet chain looped down from his belt loop. Lisa wanted one too. She breathed in his cologne, the kind with the ship on the white bottle. Sometimes she would slap some on her face when he was making breakfast. It would sting her face.

"Dad, it's Hunter. I want to be called Hunter," Lisa prompted him.

His father always let her be Hunter, even though he sometimes forgot and called her Lisa. Deep down inside Hunter knew it couldn't be easy. But he never complained just laughed when people asked him about his tomboy daughter. Both endured sneers from strangers.

Hunter hated it. Using the women's bathroom was especially traumatic; all the girls and their mothers would gasp when Hunter appeared. He didn't want to use the girl's restroom, but his dad said he had to draw the line somewhere. Hunter had to give in every time.

"Mommy, is that a boy or girl?"

"I don't know, dear, but I think IT is in the wrong bathroom."

Lisa went over to the feminine hygiene machine. She had to change her pad anyway, and it would be comical to mess with dragon lady and her brat kid, taking time to fish for a dime in her pocket. The maxi pad, along with the sock made her unconquerable, like she had a dick once she got over the initial shock. As she wiggled the pad from the machine, the lady's mouth opened wide enough to extract a tooth. Lisa frowned at their ignorance. Someday they would know she was Hunter. That she really was a boy.

Beep! Beep! The monitor woke Hunter. The drugs made everything hazy and foggy.

"Why am I all wet?" Hunter touched the dressing, the wetness soaking the bandages again. He gently rubbed the stitches slowly circling around the bloody cloth that contained his new addition, feeling the unfamiliar, welcome shape of it.

"It's a fucking miracle! I did it! Screw you, Stan!"

"Who is Stan?" Cate asked as she opened the door.

Hunter jolted his hand back. "No one important. When can I see the doctor? I have some questions."

"Tomorrow, but now we clean you up and get you some food." Cate advised. Her teeth were perfectly straight, like keys on a piano board.

"So, Hunter, may I ask you a personal question?" Cate queried, busy at work.

"Go ahead." Hunter responded.

"When did you decide to have reassignment surgery?"

"I always knew that I wasn't connected to my body. Something wasn't right. I always recognized that I wasn't female, but I didn't really understand for a long time. When I was twelve, I watched this older girl go into a grocery store with her boyfriend. I was waiting for my mom in the car. She had this long dark hair, and she kept cuddling up against his shoulder. Their hands were interlocked, and they walked like their bodies were totally connected. I was immersed in a bubble of rage and pain. That's when I identified. It paralyzed me. But I knew I would do anything to have that. To be that boyfriend. I hated my body so much."

The memory took over as Cate got breakfast ready. Hunter trapped in Lisa. Her boobs always an open invitation to be stared at. He was suffocating, like swimming in a swamp. I was spinning my wheels trying to escape my female skin, but every flight led right back to the starting point. I'm not a girl! One day, pulling out a pocketknife from her jean pocket, Lisa opened the switchblade and admired the light reflecting off the blade. Ugly thoughts barraged her. Could she cut both nipples off, scrape away the tissue that made Hunter look like Lisa, free his spirit?

Hunter whispered; his eyes closed. "I wanted to cut my breasts off." The blade was ice cold against Lisa's skin. You can do it, Lisa. One quick slice and they will be gone, and no one can touch them ever again. "But I couldn't fucking do it! I was a coward. It was so hard." He unlocked his eyes to see Cate listening intently. "But when I was older, when I could fix it, I swore I would go through every step." Hunter looked away.

Cate stretched for Hunter's hand. "You were not a coward. You were a child."

It was hard to put that unbearable weight down, even now. The helpless suffering when he knew his prayers would be unanswered. He would never go to sleep and wake up a boy. That he had to live as Lisa, that the only reply was unrequited prayers. The sobs as Lisa put the switchblade away and stared off into space, hoping somehow, some way there would be a sign from God, that he could be himself. And here he was.

Cate's body exuded a comforting warmth as she swaddled him in fresh sheets. Hunter craved the calmness she provided, but suddenly froze stiff, vulnerable, and defenseless.

"What about you Cate? What made you pursue the health field? Do you have a lot of experience with transitioning patients?" He was curious, too. She seemed to understand so well. Behind her eyes was a story he wanted to hear.

"I am just a born caretaker, Hunter. Now get some rest. Your body needs to heal." Cate's motherly character trickles through, automatically.

"I told you so much about myself! It's only fair. Besides, I'm interested." Hunter swallowed his meds with a sip of cold water and took a bite of toast.

"Maybe another time. I don't mind just listening, anyway — it's part of my job. I will check with you before I leave today."

Something was different about Cate, and he was going to find out what. For the next few hours, he faded in and out of sleep, trying to ignore the throbbing pain in his groin. The bottom surgery created unbearable pressure in his pelvis. He hoped it was normal.

Half asleep, Hunter brushed his hands absently across his chest. It was sometimes still a little weird not to have boobs anymore, but he loved the sense of freedom. He had hated his girly body and today he had finally completed the last step — he had what he always wanted. His heart beating strong sang him to sleep home at last, home at last.

In the dream, Hunter glanced down at his chest and realized he was Lisa again. The unbearable summer's heat soused the ace bandages tight against her unwanted breasts. Ensnared again!

Lisa was riding in an old rusty car. A sickly familiar smell invaded the air. It was the kind of musty stink from not having a bath for a couple days, combined with an edge of deodorant wearing off on a hot summer afternoon. Stan's stink. Lisa glimpsed over — her brother had a joint hanging out of his mouth. Stan was talking, but all Lisa could hear was noise as a familiar dread began to engulf her. A sense of imminent doom lurking. Something vile was about to happen.

"Hey, why are you so quiet? Cat got your tongue. Fetch the fishing poles and the tackle box," Stan shouted in a gravelly and impatient tone. Lisa hated how he tried to be the boss. She got out of the car and slammed the door. They started down the clay path to the big concrete wall where they always cast their lines. Lisa didn't want to sit on the wall with Stan. Lisa was always aware of his intentions.

"Hey, where are you going? Stay close. I'm not getting yelled at by Mom if you fall in the water or get all dirty."

Mom never yells at you for anything, Lisa mouthed to herself. She'll blame me. But she didn't say it.

Instead, she strategized. "I just want to check this one spot out. The fish are jumping out of the water." Lisa went as far away as she could, taking a deep breath with plenty of space between them.

"Lisa!!! Did you fucking hear me?" Lisa envisioned Stan's small pupils, the whites of his eyes red and filled with broken blood vessels. He probably had stayed up all night shooting drugs. He was still high, Lisa concluded.

Lisa stopped and turned around. Hunter dragged along in the dream, stuck as Lisa. He wanted to run, to snatch the keys to the truck and get out of there. But he hadn't done that. Lisa knew the wrath she'd face if she didn't give in.

"Hand me my pole. What's wrong with you today? You're starting to piss me off. Are you having boy problems or something?" His brother laughed and moved closer. A prickly sensation filled Lisa's stomach and glued her arms to her sides.

"Hey, can I have some of that joint?" She had to distract Stan.

Stan passed it over, his fat fingers almost covering it. Lisa tried to grab it from him while avoiding eye contact, took a long drag, almost burning her fingers.

Hunter would do anything to escape what was festering in the dismal air, but he couldn't wake up.

This was not how it was supposed to be. Lisa was sinking in quicksand, drowning, and gasping for air. She wished she would close her eyes and wake up, becoming Hunter all the way, be himself. Hunter tried to make that happen, but Lisa's skin and bones encased and cornered him.

"Lisa, wake up! Get us a beer out of the cooler," Stan snapped.

The life was slowly draining out of her as she tried dipping her fingers slowly into the ice to help her focus. Too late. She tossed a beer to her brother and opened one for herself, chugging it down to numb all the doubt and fear swirling in her head. Lisa/Hunter gulped too fast, tried to keep from plunging over the edge.

"Lisa, come over here and sit by me," Stan's voice echoed off the water.

Lisa was shaking at the thought of him touching her.

His brother seized Lisa's hand and placed it on his inner thigh. Hunter's stomach churned into knots. Lisa was trying not to tremble. Maybe she could sidetrack him.

"Hey, I just want to fish and drink this beer." Asshole. Lisa murmured. Stan gave her a dirty look and put a worm on his hook.

Stan's body tightened and tensed. He cussed and cast his line in the water. Lisa watched the line on Stan's pole disappear into the current. What was beneath the surface, and would it get away from the hook? Was there a big hungry fish it was trying to swim away from? Was it paying attention?

The car ride home was going to be unbearable. When she shut down Stan's advances there was always hell to pay.

"The fish aren't biting today. I'm ready to go." He started to reel his line in. She left hers in the water. Stan purposely cut across Lisa's path and almost tangled their lines up. Stan would ruin her good time at any cost.

"We just got here. I'm not ready to go yet," Lisa pleaded.

"Well, isn't that too fucking bad. Did you drive? No, so pack your shit."

"Please, I really want to stay for a while. It's peaceful here."

Stan paused, finally unlocking his sealed lips, exposing the fake silver tooth. "Well, maybe you could convince me to stay a while longer."

Hunter's stomach constricted as he underwent Stan's eyes raking over Lisa's body. Wake up, Hunter! Wake up!

Lisa decided. If Stan cornered her in the car the rape would be twice as bad. At least at the lake she had some control. Lisa could say a hiker is coming or someone else to fish. And Stan would have to hurry up or stop. Either way it was a small victory. Maybe just maybe after he was done, she could drink a beer and fish in peace. So, she —

Hunter woke from his dream shouting, sweaty and claustrophobic. The IV coiled his arm, so he extended over with his other hand and withdrew the imported tube. Just then, the door opened.

"Hunter, what are you doing? You're bleeding all over!" Cate shrieked.

The warm liquid began to travel down his arm. He saw that his gown was stained with blood, but he didn't care. He wasn't safe. "I need to get out of here!" Hunter tried to pluck the rest of the IV out of his arm.

Cate gently put her hand over his, as he lay back, suddenly still. "Sometimes when we have no place to go it's better to stay. Here, put the cold cloth on your forehead."

"Crazy — crazy dreams." Hunter admitted.

"You were saying the name Stan again. I heard you yelling when I passed by the door. Do you want to talk about it?"

"Old demons." Hunter handed Cate the cloth. "Stan is my brother."

"I assume you don't get along with him?" Cate asked delicately.

"Stan is an evil bastard." Hunter remarked, jaw tight. "An abusive drug addict. He preys on women and teenage girls. My mother protected him. She didn't want his shortcomings to reflect on her parenting skills."

"Where was your father?"

Hunter closed his eyes, searching for the right words. "Divorced. But my father was my light. He loved me for who I was — am. We loved the outdoors, planting flowers and vegetables... He taught me to..." Hunter shook his head. "Look, I talk too much. You probably hear too many stories."

"Another hat I wear is therapist. I enjoy listening. I want to know about you." She expertly checked his IV.

"Well, I like to listen, too. Tell me something about yourself - anything." Hunter's emerald eyes danced with anticipation. This would be a welcome distraction. And he was sure her story would be fascinating. He bounced back into his skin, fully himself.

Cate checked his dressing, then busied herself with the beeping monitor at his bedside, appearing to collect her thoughts. Finally, she sat by the bed.

She stared off into space and seemed to drift. The mood was shifting, like an eerie darkness when the sun disappears behind the moon. Like an eclipse.

She surveyed out the window. "Sometimes, I let things consume me. I did, anyway. For a little while. Work, family, friends. It's hard to explain. For a long time, my life was very lonely."

"So how did you come out of it?"

Cate concentrated on him with a glimmer of optimism. "Well, let's just say, I think we're more alike than you know. And I'm grateful for patients like you! I'll check back later." Her eyes were two bright mysterious lights, sparks from the bottom of the blue ocean, secrets waiting to be discovered. She was mesmerizing. Hunter hated to see her go.

CHAPTER 2

On the drive home from work, Cate fiddled with the radio to stay awake. Work was busy today.

She rummaged into the pocket of her uniform to touch the pills she had stashed that day. "Now I can just have a nice hot bath and relax."

Cate plowed into her driveway and saw her cat Smokey in his usual spot, head butting the curtains to peek outside. Cate had found him abandoned in a dumpster, covered in fleas. Truth be told, Smokey saved her that day as much as she saved him. Cate understood the anguish of abandonment. Growing up in the foster care system, she soon learned if she didn't conform to whatever predetermined norm created by her foster family, she would be kicked out, like trash. Smokey wouldn't be overlooked like that, not on her watch.

"Hello, Smokey, how was your day?" Cate stroked his soft fur and picked up the papers and other clutter that he knocked down in protest whenever she was at work. "I'm home now, boy! Are you hungry?"

Smokey's relentless weaving and signature eight loop causes Cate to lose her balance. "You're talkative today. Slow down I'm getting your food." Even dirty and lost, Cate had seen how beautiful he was, his coat was crème colored with black patches intertwined throughout his coat. His majestic blues eyes blinked thanks and he dug into his dinner.

Cate uncovered a bottle of whiskey and a glass, started her bath water, and ran her fingers under the faucet to test the temperature. The water splashing hurled her back to that horrific day.

"Come on Michael, we need to get cleaned-up for dinner." She tucked her son into the tub, but she was distracted, thinking about getting high. She had nodded off while he was still in the water. His splashing and frantic cries woke her up, as she barely made it there to save him. Her ex had threatened to call the police. Cate had to promise she would go into treatment. Treatment. That was the first time.

She poured a drink and gulped back the guilt, slipped out of her clothes and into the water. Cate swallowed both pills. Smokey pawed opened the door and jumped up on the toilet. He had been there through it all, Cate sighed. And he still loved her. Silly cat.

From Cate's painful divorce to a couple stints in rehab, he always welcomed her home. And people say cats are not loyal. We're a lot alike, Smokey. He begged for a scratch, tiptoeing on the bathtub ledge like a tight rope. The pills and alcohol give everything a welcome haze as she relaxed in the water.

But unwelcome thoughts intruded. Cate suspected that they were on to her at work. Donna had her spies watching. She had to be more careful.

Cate found her towel and wiped the moisture off the mirror. It was starting all over again. The addiction was creeping in like a weed strangling carefully arranged tulips. She made her way to the closet, ignoring the pile of men's suits, faded jeans, work boots, and flannel shirts on the floor in the back, strictly segregated from her own feminine wardrobe. They were better off left in their corner. Smokey circled the cast-off clothes, gave them a sniff, nestled into them.

"Why would you be loyal to him, Smokey?" she scoffed. Refilling her cocktail, she paused at the full-length mirror on the bathroom door. She slowly ran her fingers over her own scars and relived each incision. Overall, she was pleased. Turning forty was challenging and through it all she had remained in good shape. Men have it easy, she recited to herself, they don't judge themselves on this perfectionist scale.

Cate slowly buffed cream into her scars. She wanted them to evaporate. The only connection she had to them was a life she had never chosen. Cate retrieved her silky pink robe and made her way to her bedroom. Smokey was waiting for her on the unmade bed.

She investigated his alert face. "I met an interesting man today, Smokey. His name is Hunter."

Smokey purred. They fell asleep together.

The night slid by. The new shift of nurses drifted in and out, not half as captivating, or solicitous as Cate had been. Between dreamy thoughts of Cate and interruptions from regular vitals checks and pills, Hunter dozed, occasionally picking up a book or writing in his journal before he fell asleep again.

Early in the morning, a child's voice outside Hunter's window awakened him.

"Tie down the fishing poles, kid!" A tailgate slammed. The sound rattled Hunter's subconscious. Hunter floated weightless into the past again.

"Stan, do you have a lighter for this joint?"

He spat into the water. "In my pocket," he mumbles, clearly irritated.

"Well, can I, have it?"

"I'm busy. Come fucking GET IT!"

Lisa/Hunter was pissed off as she set the pole down and started to walk over the sharp rocks and sinkholes of mud that filled her tennis shoes. I will get my shoes good and dirty and maybe this time, mom will realize you're to blame, jerk! She spotted some tiny fish huddled together in a school. Sensing her shadow, they swam away with purpose. Smart fish, she thought, swim far away! Nothing here but getting caught.

Hunter sank deep into the dream, once again descending into Lisa's body, and Lisa's fear.

When she arrived at his spot something was wrong. Stan rotated his right pocket toward Lisa. She would have to get it herself. But then he spun and twisted, causing Lisa to fall into the mud and lose one of her tennis shoes. He gripped her hard, lifting Lisa's feet a few inches off the muddy ground.

"Listen, I came out here to relax and have a good time. So, that means we are going to do what I want to do. Where the fuck is your shoe? Aww shit you're dirty! You're damn clumsy for a girl!" He burrowed his dirty fingernails into her skin. Lisa knew what that meant; she tried to break away but slipped in the mud again. Stan jammed her arm behind her back and hauled her up sharply. She tried not to cry.

"Pack our stuff. We're going home. I'll deal with you later."

Lisa flashed on a fantasy, pushing Stan into the river. He wasn't a great swimmer. He would never make it back to the shore. No one would miss him except mom and soon enough he would turn up, snagged in a bunch of rocks. The beads of perspiration ran down her back and soaked into the boy's underwear that her brother teased her about, mercilessly.

"Why do you wear those? You're not a boy, you're a girl. No man will ever want you—that is disgusting. You're a mess, WEIRDO!"

"Shut up," Lisa would mutter, and duck her head, but she wanted to say, You're the weirdo. I am a boy. I'm Hunter. Lisa gathered the fishing gear slowly. Her mind was wandering. The anger bubbled inside her chest and spilled over into her heart, like boiling water on a stove, too much heat.

The car ride home was in silence. Stan's knuckles on the steering wheel turned white, holding and twitching. Lisa's head was pounding. Stan was going to make good on his threat. She tried to prepare herself. While Stan was unloading the truck, Lisa went right to her room and changed her muddy clothes. She closed the door and put some music on, trying to escape into different thoughts. Someday I'll be far away from here and none of this will matter.

 Stan's heavy boots scratched down the hall, announcing his entrance. He slammed around in the kitchen, looking for a snack. Maybe it will blow over. Slowly, she started to drift into sleep, pushing away visions of Stan glaring with his silver tooth shimmering in the sunlight. His nicotine-stained hands all over her telling Lisa that it's OK, no one needs to know. That no one would understand their special bond that he created for them.

"It's our secret," Stan sneered and hissed in Hunter's dreams, disguising himself as the biblical snake tempting Eve to the forbidden fruit.

Then he was in Lisa's room, the door creaking open, the glowing red tip of a cigarette a hot point in the darkness. Cigarette smoke filled the room with dread and apprehension.

"Hey, want a cig?" Stan offers.

"No, I'm OK—really tired." The liquor on his breath spread throughout the room like wildfire. Terror set in and held Lisa to her mattress.

"You know that I really care about you, don't you?" Stan sat close, captured Lisa's hand, and placed it on his genitals. She sprung her hand away, but her brother was stronger. He began to unzip his jeans. He didn't have underwear on, and he was growing larger. She tried to run away.

"C'mon. I know you like it. No one understands you like I do. You make everything better, babe." Stan was a manipulator. Next, he would talk about how bad his childhood was. How lonely he had become. His sense of entitlement was revolting.

Hunter's life wasn't a bed of roses, either. It really didn't matter, though. To Stan, Lisa was disposable. So, Lisa shot back into herself, becoming future Hunter. Her head inflated like a balloon loose from the string, soaring away from earth and all its Stan-made tricks and restrictions.

Future Hunter. That's me, Hunter said to himself. I'm safe now. But the trepidation was descending, just like when Stan finished, always reminding Lisa, "Remember, Child Services would take you away if they knew what you were doing. We have a good relationship, don't we? You don't want to go into a home? They would blame you. And you make it happen, Lisa, you know that. You know that, right?"

More than once, Lisa/Hunter would think, desperately, going away might be OK after all. But no — everything he went through as Lisa brought him to this point of becoming whole. Becoming himself. He had always been there, inside. Lisa was part of him.

Sometimes it seemed like a vicious circle, the bad memories never ending. I wish it would go away; Hunter muttered to himself.

Hunter distracted himself imagining Cate's shift must be starting soon. On the tree branches outside his window, he studied a red cardinal sitting on a tree limb. Another bird joined him. They must have a nest nearby. The male fed his mate, placing his beak in hers.

Now that's love. It reminded him of Susie and how much she enjoyed bird watching. He fingered the scar on his right forearm, visualizing the night they broke up. The night he decided to finally transition physically.

"The point that I'm trying to make is, Susie, I would be there for you no matter what."

"Oh, really? I call bullshit, Hunter!" Susie's hands went to her hips. "So, if I woke up one day and stated that I wanted to become a man you would back me up?"

"It doesn't work that way." Hunter said sarcastically.

"Exactly! That is what I was thinking when you told me!"

"I have been this way from day one, Susie, and you knew it."

She didn't want to hear it, though. Her whole life would change because she was in love with Hunter, and she wanted him to be Lisa. "I'm a lesbian, Lisa, and so are you. You have always been very irrational and impulsive. You need to think about this—this is affecting both of us. Not just you." Susie's eyebrows rose and she suddenly looked so certain. Hunter despised that arrogance, that smug idea that her assumptions made sense for everyone.

Hunter couldn't contain himself anymore. "Do you know what it's like to live in a bubble? To be stuck like you're in a constant shell. To loathe every man that walks down the street because you want that confidence on the inside, but your outside isn't that way? All you care about is keeping up with the neighbors, being the perfect super femme, dressed in every new fashion trend. You don't listen! You don't care!"

Walking away from her he knew he couldn't live in this body anymore. The pictures of Lisa and Susie, grinning on the mantle, seemed to mock him. He threw the frame across the room, and it scattered into a million shards. I hated that picture of me anyway. He slammed into the hallway and his reflection, somewhere between Hunter and Lisa, but still so feminine, bounced off the mirror. Drawing his right hand back he had smashed the mirror shattering it instantly. A few jagged pieces lodged inside his arm, slicing him open.

Susie had run out the door never to be heard from again. He had to take himself to the clinic for stitches, his arm in an old towel. His heart was breaking over Susie, but he was thankful she had left. He needed to surface. He was better off without her. His journey as a man was meant to be his alone.

Life really was ironic. Hunter hated Stan, but when he was Lisa, she wanted to become strong like Stan, like the men who had hurt her all those years. Sure, only the physical aspect of them not the violent side. But cornered, he had so much rage it was confusing. Even now, Hunter only knew a few men who were truly gentle. The kind of men that women desired. He wanted to become a passionate man, giving his lover everything, making her safe. He knew what women wanted because he once was a woman, technically. It did give him an edge, he decided. And now, he was fully male. Finally. Could he do it right?

The hospital room door opened, and a sultry silhouette appeared - Cate. She had a sexy and confident energy. He would love to have someone like her to take care of.

"Lost in your thoughts, Hunter?" Cate spoke with enthusiasm. "Maybe I should offer you a penny."

Hunter grinned. There was something about this woman that seemed familiar.

"I think my thoughts are worth more than a penny." Hunter shook his memory of Susie off and looked Cate over as she checked his vitals.

"Hey, you never told me what you do for a living?" Cate repositioned Hunter to clean his bandages. His scars look like a ground war, long slits connected and disappearing, stitched together in a whole different landscape. Cate mapped every intimate scar as she waited for his answer.

"I'm a writer." Hunter declared.

"Really! What do you write about?"

"Mostly fiction, but I'm writing a memoir at the moment."

"Putting your life under a public microscope. I don't know about that," Cate trailed off.

"It's my way of understanding everything. I would love to write a book about your life, Cate." Hunter implied.

"Why would you want to do that?"

"Your eyes are so deep, so full of sadness and intelligence. I want to know your story." Hunter smiled lightly.

"I'm sure yours is more interesting than mine. Now eat your breakfast, hand-some. We will chat later." And just like that Cate floated away. As he watched her go, Hunter promised himself he would find a way for her to trust him. Maybe we can help each other.

Cate counted each line on the newly buffed hospital floor. It was a distraction she had invented as a small child to pass the time, sitting outside the Child Protection Services administrative office on the faded wooden bench, waiting to find out where she would be placed next. It kept her from imagining the next disappointment. Most of her foster parents only wanted a check. And they let Cate know it.

As she counted tiles down the corridor, she visualized following one set of foster parents walking down a long, white, dimly lit hallway. No one was talking. Cate was uneasy and her foster parents kept glancing tensely at her. The current father's eyes were cold as steel and lifeless, looking right at her but not registering her as human. The mother avoided all eye contact. Through the large oak doors at the end, where she stood with familiar hopeless silence, listening to their strained, defensive voices, self-righteous and cruel.

"We refuse to deal with this child's erratic and disobedient behavior. We have been generous opening our home. Even been patient. Every option has been exhausted. But it is time for other arrangements to be made." Cate's foster father's neck muscles were bulging, although he spoke quietly.

She hated thinking of him as her dad but underwent more grief than relief. She had already lost her biological father, a man she met only when he became sick, and she had recently learned of her mother's death. It seemed there was nowhere good left to go.

In and out of foster homes until finally Cate officially became a ward of the state. Always being thrown away. The story was Cate's biological father was on the road as a traveling salesman, leaving Cate with her mother, who wandered. Cate spent most of her days with her mom's sister or the neighbors until the state stepped in.

She had sworn it wouldn't happen to her family. She needed to fix her relationship with her son, Michael, before it was too late. He wore his resentment like body armor, deflecting anything that he didn't want to deal with. We are more alike than he realizes. Cate sighed to herself as she slipped a couple more pills in her pocket.

Hunter couldn't decide if he was more hungry or excited, aware that Cate would be making her lunchtime rounds soon. Sure, the stunning nurse was easy on the eyes, but it was so much more than that. Hunter wanted to pierce her protective professionalism. She had a depth that kept surprising him.

Outside his window, if he sat up, he could watch the families coming and going, trying to figure out their stories to entertain himself. For some, their faces were so imprinted with pain it halted them in time. One little boy played in the grass at the edge of the lot. His mom was talking on her cell phone. His toy soldier was tucked behind a mound of sand, ready to fight off the imaginary enemy.

That kid was a natural daredevil leaping off the mound of sand. It was reminiscent of the Evel Knievel Christmas, his favorite when he was known as Lisa. Not everything was terrible. That morning, Lisa ran up the stairs to see if Santa had visited. A line of presents was under the tree - everything she asked for, a surprise because her family struggled to put food on the table. Fleetwood Mac albums, the shining Evel Knievel motorcycle, even G.I. Joe. Christmas day they played all day with their toys, no boring church to pray the day away.

But these moments were short lived. Stan always made sure of that. That year started out so well, but within a few hours, Stan had broken all her things, like he wanted to break her spirit. He and his friends loved to play tricks on her, to scare her, or corner her. Now that she was developing, they became more spiteful, and Hunter seemed a faraway impossibility. As winter turned to spring, Stan and Jimmie planned a new prank, one she couldn't see through, one that put Lisa in a very dangerous position.

"Hey Lisa, how is it going?" Jimmie catechized with his lip curled up like Elvis. All the girls had a crush on him touching his rippling biceps. The boys on the block feared him. Jimmie was athletic and stocky. His coal dark hair a black stallion's mane. His chipped tooth made him look virile. Lucky bastard! Lisa muttered.

"I'm fine, Jimmie. Where is Sara?"

"She isn't here, but she did give me a letter to give you." He presented an envelope out of his back pocket, folded in half, and covered with sweat. "Sara told me to give it to her when you have finished writing. So, when you are done give it to me."

Lisa uprooted the letter and hurried around to the big oak tree across the street. She tore it open, her hands trembling and anxious sweat dripping down her back.

> *Lisa, I've been thinking about something. I must finally tell you. I think about you all the time. I know that I should be thinking about boys, but they don't move me like your spirit does. I love the way you look at me. I think you identify the same way. Would you come over one weekend and stay with me? We can explore this together. Let me know!*
>
> *Sara*

Lisa's mind ran wild in all four directions. Could this be happening? Finally, someone understood her. Lisa folds the letter up and ran home as fast as she could. It was almost as if a fog was lifting, the sun bouncing off the leaves and beaming across her face. As Lisa approached her house she saw Stan outside, smoking a cigarette, clearly looking for her. She snuck around the house and used the back door – she wouldn't let him ruin this moment!

Lisa went into her bedroom and found some paper from her desk drawer. Sara, I'm flattered that you care about me, and return my crush on you. I'm not interested in the boys, either. In fact, I'd rather become one. Anyway, I gladly accept your invitation. Let me know what weekend works for you! Lisa.

Heavy footsteps barreled down the stairs and she knew it was Stan. Lisa tried to hide the letter, but it was too late.

"What do we have here?" Stan sneered as he seized the letter from Lisa's hand. "I'm not interested in boys, either. I'd rather become one. What the fuck shit is this?"

Lisa tried to take the letter back. "It's none of your fucking business! Why don't you just leave me alone?" Stan blocked her in the doorway.

"Now you listen to me, you sick little bitch! You think you have a chance with that hot number, Sara? You better wake the fuck up! You don't want to be a boy

— all you need is some real dick! As far as your friend, Sara? Well, send her my way! I'll show her what a man can do."

Lisa's limbs were hot as red ash. Rage pulsed through her body. Now was not the time to fight; she needed to get her letter to Sara. She pushed past Stan, and he brushed against her, his penis hard. She had to fight the urge to scratch his eyes out. He just smirked and watched her runaway.

Someday he will pay; I'll knock his teeth out! Lisa dodged the darkness around her as she ran towards Jimmie's house. It must just be Stan's bad energy. She saw Jimmie out front, his dark black mane shining off his dark sunglasses.

Jimmie was friendly, even excited. "Do you have the letter? Sara is in the garage."

"Yes, I'll take it to her myself."

Jimmie was walking beside Lisa. The clouds were gray and billowy and the static electricity from an incoming storm was thick and hovering. As they approached the open garage door, Sara was propped up against the building smoking a cigarette and laughing. She was so beautiful, and she would be Lisa's soon!

Jimmie knocked on the open garage door and Larry waved them in, avoiding eye contact with Lisa, but looking her over when he thought she couldn't see. Larry's garage was their little hideaway, the setting of many summer parties. Smoking weed, drinking beer, or doing shots of whiskey passed the long, hot nights. Lisa admired Jimmie; he commanded respect but was also fair. His god-like body was what she wanted hers to become.

"What's up, Jimmie?" Larry's molasses-colored eyes were undressing Lisa. She ignored him.

"Nothing. Let us in." All the neighbor boys were in awe of Jimmie and a little scared of his strength.

"I need a drink, Jimmie. I'll be back."

Lisa really wanted a minute to breathe. Sara was in a corner by the keg, talking to some girls from school. Her long brown barrel curls had a tint of red streaks, from her Irish mother. Big green eyes shone as dark as the moss on the rocks in the thick of summer. As Lisa walked, Sara signaled her over.

"Hi Lisa, how are you?"

"I'm OK. How is school going?"

Lisa really didn't want to talk about school, but she figured it was better than running away before she delivered her letter.

"OK, I guess… Algebra is a pain in my ass…"

"Well, I've something for you." Lisa cut her off out of nervousness. She surrendered the letter much like a student at the end of a test, shaking a little.

Sara tilted her head to one side. Halting the red cup filled to the brim with keg beer.

"What's this?"

"The letter you wanted."

Sara unfolds the letter, and her face began to twist into a confused frown, as her eyes scanned the first few lines. She threw the note to the ground.

"What the fuck is this about?"

"Jimmie gave your letter to me, and you told me that you wanted me to write you back." Lisa cradled her stomach to prevent her from retching.

"I didn't write you a letter, and if I did it wouldn't have sex stuff in it. I have a boyfriend, Lisa! What the hell is wrong with you?"

The garage began to close in. Lisa's heart was slowly squeezing her lungs with the familiar feeling of betrayal and shame. All the boys on the block and Stan, they wouldn't leave her alone!

Jimmie strutted over and bent down to pick up the letter.

"I gladly accept your invitation. Let me know what weekend works for you!" Jimmie read aloud.

"What is this bullshit, Lisa?" Jimmie screamed, taking a few steps back. "Everyone told me that you liked Sara, but I defended you! And now you write her a love letter?"

"You lied to me, Jimmie!"

"Everyone told me. Dressing like a boy. Walking and talking like one—it's disgusting!"

"Well, your friends didn't seem to think it was when they were trying to force themselves on me!" Lisa shot back.

"I call bullshit, Lisa! Stay away from us!"

Cate's perfume brought Hunter fully back from the memory just as he was beginning to slip into the present. Hunter's face flushed with pleasure as he caught a scent that only belonged to a woman.

"The sun is blinding this time of day." Cate marched over to shut the blinds.

"No! Please keep it open. I like to people watch. It helps to pass the time."

"Of course, you're a writer. You know, I could bring you in a notepad and pen so you could write down some of your thoughts. It might help to inspire you. I will be right back!"

Before Hunter could utter a word, Cate was out the door and on a mission. Some writing materials would be nice, Hunter reasoned to himself. His bandages shifted, signs of new life.

He glided his fingers under the bandage, explored his new member with his right hand, finally freed from needles and tubes. His soft pubic hair was growing in, prickly like a porcupine. But he stroked it, – manhood, fleshy and real.

I did it! I fucking did it! Hunter erupted with excitement. He spent some time gently examining his new body. The tissue was a little sore and sensitive still, and the stiches marked the edges, like an intricate jig saw puzzle.

But then, his celebration turned dark, remembering Lisa's longing, and the bullies that exploited her. If Lisa was a freak, of course they would have to treat her like one. And if they could, fix her good.

"Hey Lisa." Larry called her over on a lazy August afternoon. "Do you want to come in the garage and drink a beer?"

It was hot and Lisa was bored. She knew what Larry wanted. She didn't care. "Sure."

Larry went to the ice cooler and fetched two Pabst Blue Ribbons. He put on Fleetwood Mac, nervously popped the caps, and handed her one.

"Where is everyone?"

"Sara went out shopping." Larry chugged his beer.

After a few beers, Lisa began to think he and Sara could be twins. The walls started to come down, she became reckless. "Want to sit by me Larry?" She wanted to make the rules this time, see what she could stir up.

"Do you want to play strip poker?" Lisa recommended shuffling the cards on the faded oak table.

"Great!" Larry's eagerness was written all over his face. But twenty minutes later, Lisa was still fully dressed.

Larry was suddenly uncomfortable. "Why are all my clothes off? You still have all yours." Larry covered himself up with a couch pillow.

"I'm really good at cards." Lisa dismissed him with a wave of her hand. She had learned how to stack the deck from Stan. "Lie back. Let me look at you."

Larry sat back blushing, and Lisa took the pillow away to admire his lanky body. Kissing him, imagining he was Sara, enjoying his vulnerability, she relished her power. He and his sister were both athletic and lean. Lisa closed her eyes and imagined Larry's body was Sara's, committed to memory from quick peeks in the changing rooms in gym class. At the same time, she was trying to understand what he was encountering, with his boy's physique strong and weak at the same time.

"Sara, I want to kiss you," Lisa angled in.

"What?" Larry said in shock jumping up off the couch.

"Nothing I was..."

Larry rushed to get dressed. "Go home, Lisa. You're still a freak!"

"Fuck you, Larry!" Lisa slammed the door. What did I do? I'm so embarrassed. Lisa avoided Larry for a couple days, hoping things would smooth over. She wanted to try again to explore his frame and compare how she wanted hers and fantasize. Next time I will keep quiet.

Hunter gently massaged himself. His new penis was still sore, but a spikey sensation calmed him. It was amazing to finally be like Larry. If Sara saw him now, she wouldn't be disgusted. And Larry – well, he'd probably be a little jealous.

Cate squeezed his shoulder, surprising him. "I'm back! I found you a spiral notebook and a couple ball point pens. Hunter, is everything OK?"

"Yes," Hunter cleared his dry throat. He moved his hand away from his groin. Had she caught him?

"Is it that Stan again?" Cate dragged up a chair and crossed her dancer like legs. Hunter caught a glimpse of her slip, black and lacey. His fingertips traced his lips. Stifling the words forming in his throat.

"Just another skeleton in my closet."

"Do you want to talk about it?" Cate blurted out.

"Maybe over dinner?"

"Are you asking me out?" Cate countered.

Hunter reacted immediately, to not lose his nerve. "Do you want to do a writing exercise with me?"

"I do have other patients…"

"It won't take long." Hunter cut her off.

"For two minutes, open all your senses and describe them to me. Use this room and anything outside your window. You take the first turn."

"Hunter," Cate's cheeks became rosy.

"OK, I'll go first. Will you write it down? I can see… an old oak tree outside my window. I hear squeaky shoes on the newly buffed floors in the hallway. I taste the chemicals in this water. I feel deep scars on my chest. And lastly, I can smell your skin cream." Hunter winked.

Cate tucked her blonde curl behind her ear. "Not fair. I'm not a writer."

"It's not a contest. Try." Hunter nodded.

"I can see how long your eyelashes are." Cate laughed. "It makes me wonder if they are false eyelashes. I hear the annoying beeping from the monitors. I can smell the mowed grass from outside on my shoes."

"That's great Cate! Keep going."

"I can touch my necklace; it gives me comfort. I can taste my lipstick." Cate raised her long-manicured fingers to her lips.

The sexual tension in the air was thick and Cate knew it. "Ummm... Here are your pain pills. I need to go."

Hunter couldn't speak. He watched her leave and swallowed his pain medicine. The pen smelled like her hand lotion. Hunter swayed it under his nose. He admired her precise penmanship in the notebook. Cate was a work of art. I will find out her mysteries.

CHAPTER 3

Cate took a deep breath and rested against Hunter's door, before moving briskly down the hall. She was shaking inside from being around the opiates. And Hunter was getting under her skin. She was already in trouble; now she was flirting with a patient! Down, girl!

She was dizzy and unsteady droplets of perspiration attached to her upper lip. As she slipped into the bathroom, she reached into her pocket and fingered the two stolen pills. The stall door lock was broken. Her hands were clammy and shaky.

The narcotics slowly went down her throat, so soothing and familiar. She didn't even need water. Cate had to take her morning pill too, or her body chemistry would be out of whack. But it would have been a red flag if anyone found it on her. The morning pill resembled the narcotics same color. So ironic! If they only knew...

As she came out of the stall, she dumped her purse on the floor, and the rest of her pill stash rolled across the floor. The door creaked open, and Cate's co-worker strolled in.

"Cate, are you OK?"

"Yes! I'm fine, just a little clumsy."

"Well, let me help you!"

Cate was frantic and moving around to gather up the evidence before her secret was revealed. This would end her nursing career for sure.

"Cate, what's going on here?"

"It's not what you think. I was prescribed those for the pain in my feet from standing all day." Cate's face went white.

"Cate, it's really none of my business but as your colleague I'm bound by a code of ethics to disclose. I'm sorry." She turned and dashed away; the evidence was still clutched in her hand.

The sturdy sink supported Cate's weight. This was it; she was done. As she headed down the hall, every person she saw seemed to be staring at her. There would be havoc soon, she was certain.

"Fuck it, if I'm going down, let's go out with a bang." Cate staggered a little, her legs rubbery and thick, as if she were fleeing a sinking ship. She had to get outside; the hospital walls were melting, and the floor was dropping out from underneath her.

She positioned herself so she could see the automatic doors, looking for her supervisor, the inevitable chopping block and her neck was on display. She had tried so hard to hold it together. One moment of clumsiness might cost her everything. Cate found the last pill and popped it into her mouth. The edges of the tablet scraped her throat and almost came back up.

Part of her didn't care that she was running out of time. Life was hard enough, but when her own son disowned her, everything got harder. All she could hear was Michael yelling as he left the house with a suitcase. Why would he blame her for every fucking thing that was wrong in his life? Michael walks in the path of the Lord now so he couldn't be bothered with a sinner. Self-righteous, self-absorbed, little prick! Cate muttered under her breath.

Part of her was desperate to keep her job. "I've got to get back to work. Maybe they'll give me another chance."

Cate ducked in through the doors, peeked inside Hunter's window and shoved down an overwhelming urge to confess everything to him. Instead, she made her way back to the bathroom. She swallowed another pill. Act normal. Act normal. In the stall, she heard the bathroom door swing open, and the clacking sound of heels on the tile floor. The same co-worker, one of Donna's spies.

"Cate? Cate are you in here?"

She adjusted herself and opened the stall door. "Yes, I'm here."

"Donna is waiting for you. She wants to speak with you."

"About?" She knew but thought if she could stall for five minutes, she could stay still, talk her way out of it.

"I'll tell Donna you'll be down shortly."

As she made her way to the office, she snuck into Hunter's room to tell him she would be taking a few days off.

"I'm here to check on you. It looks like you need some cleaning up. Just relax, I know you're sore." As Cate began to peel back Hunter's bandages, she couldn't help but be intrigued with all the scars on his body. She had hoped to stay with him throughout recovery. She worried about his pain physically and most of all, emotionally. Most people had no idea the courage it takes to completely recreate yourself. She was close to tears.

Her therapist would sometimes ask her, "What do you want out of life, Cate?" She had to really think about it. The standard answer in society was to be happy, right? Cate couldn't fathom that. She didn't know how to be happy. She wanted to be down in the trenches working, helping, pushing. It's what she identified with. Happy was too much to ask for, but maybe she could learn to use her experience, maybe find someone who could even love her flaws, if anyone really understood how much strength it took to become her.

"Are you OK, Cate? You seem so far away," Hunter's voice riddled with concern.

"I'll be fine, thank you. So, going home tomorrow, right?" Cate tinkered with the monitors. Trying to avoid telling him that this would be their last visit.

"Yes," Hunter replied with apprehension in his voice. "Will the doctor talk to me tomorrow?"

"Yes, before you are discharged. I bet you're chomping at the bit to get home."

"Well, to be honest, I'm a little frightened." Hunter looked away from her gaze.

"Listen, you're strong and have come too far to quit now. You'll be fine, I know it! I need to finish my rounds. I'll see you later."

Cate found her ink pen behind her ear and wrote something down on a piece of paper. She placed it in Hunter's coat pocket, pretending to tuck something away in the closet, and ducked out the door. Seeing Hunter had helped her shake off some of the fear. She would not let Donna take away everything she had worked for. That's all this was – a setback.

"Hello Donna. You wanted to see me?" Cate spoke firmly and precisely.

"I'm not going to beat around the bush. It's has been brought to my attention that you might be using drugs again. Also, the dispensatory is coming up short on its count. I'm placing you on a suspension pending an investigation. Do you have anything to say?"

Cate wanted to speak up and defend herself but saw Donna's hard face and stayed silent. Now wasn't the time. She had blown it – but maybe all of this would pass if she didn't make it worse by getting defensive.

"No."

"You can go get your things. I'll be in touch. Cate, I hope we are wrong. You're a good nurse."

As Cate left the office she was surprised by a great sense of relief. Whatever the outcome was, she would survive. The last pill was kicking in, too. Her head was drifting off her body and she was beginning to disappear like dew on wet grass at the first sunrise. Who cared that each person she passed avoided her eyes. She knew her story had spread instantly in the gossip mill.

As Cate gathered her things, a picture of Michael dropped onto the floor. All her memories began to flood her mind, almost suffocating her. Guilt. Shame. Rage. She had to get to a safe place.

Driving home in the rain settled her down a little. She had to focus, and all she wanted to do was curl up with Smokey. But Hunter kept returning to her mind. Would they talk again? Would he hear why she didn't come back? Would he still want to hear her story?

Smokey was already waiting in the window.

As she slowly undressed Smokey darted over her feet and into the closet. "Give it up, Smokey. It's been a bad day." As Cate burrowed into bed, the weight of the day bled deep into her bones. "Oh, Cate, what have you done?"

The next morning Hunter waited to meet the doctor and be discharged. Every squeak on the hallway floor, his heart would skip a beat hoping to see Cate's angelic face. As the clock slowly ticked away, Hunter had a feeling he wouldn't see her. Damn, I should have asked her for her number.

Finally, white shoes flashed under the door and a new nurse came in, carrying a bandage kit.

"Where is Cate today?" Hunter's face crammed with apprehension.

"She isn't here. I'm going to get you cleaned up so the doctor can come in and talk to you."

Hunter didn't like this one. She was rough, efficient but cold. Cate had spoiled him. Nothing could compare to her professionalism, elegance, and wit. He skimmed her notes, running his finger over her flowing handwriting.

Then, a short middle-aged man with salt-and-pepper, surprisingly thick hair parted down the side came in. "Hunter. Hello, I'm Doctor Thatcher. You're going home today and I'm sure that you have questions. Lie back, let's have a look."

There was a long pause. Hunter started to worry. "Is everything all right?"

Dr. Thatcher nodded. "You have some swelling and bruising which is to be expected. But you're healing nicely. We can give you an anti-bacterial cream for the redness. Apply it a couple times a day. Also, I can prescribe some pain pills - take them every four to six hours."

After a few minutes, he cleaned the stitches and applied a larger dressing.

"Everything is where it should be. You're ready to go home! Now what questions do you have for me?" The doctor sat down on the swivel stool and rolled over to Hunter's bed.

"How long before I can use the bathroom comfortably?"

"It will be sore for a while, and you need to clean the whole area afterwards, but there isn't any reason to hesitate." The doctor scribbled some notes on his writing pad.

"Will I be able to perform sexually?"

"Good question. I would wait a bit, but yes, you will eventually sustain an erection. I will send home some instructions and literature to read so you can understand how to move into intimacy gradually."

Hunter pursed his lips. He couldn't think of anything else.

The doctor stood up brusquely. "OK, then. I will have the nurse come to get you. She will bring you discharge papers to sign. If you have any questions or concerns, give me a call. We will do a follow up in a month."

It all seemed strangely anti-climactic. Hunter had to take a cab home; he lived across town. Snow began to fall, blanketing the window with the uncertainty of the outside world. Apartment buildings and houses blurred behind the flurries, like a moving picture, as he crossed the bridge to his neighborhood. Susie was on his mind; if things had been different, she would have picked him up. But they would never reconcile now. When he reached into his pocket to pay the fare, a small piece of paper fell onto his shoe.

In Cate's precise penmanship, it said: When you are home and you need a friend, call me. Cate. And there was her number. Hunter's mouth gaped open with bewilderment.

He couldn't stop humming as he put his clothes away and watered his plants. Cate wanted him to call! The chemistry between them was undeniable.

Cate frantically paced the kitchen floor. Smokey bounced after each footstep in perfect unison, wrapping his tail around her feet. But Cate was in a foul mood. Her confidence was slowly disappearing. It was clear everyone was against her. An overturned liquor bottle had spilled on the trash littering the table. Dirty dishes filled the sink and leftover Chinese containers cluttered the counter.

Above the fridge, she found some hidden pills. She absconded with another bottle and retreated to the couch, holding the pills tightly in her fist. She shoved unpaid bills aside and set the bottle down. A business card fell to the floor.

"Paul Williams." She said out loud. "Maybe I should reach out."

Her NA sponsor had recovered after living on skid row, losing his family, job, house, and even considering suicide. When a police officer found him and took him to a NA meeting, he completely changed his life. Paul was an NA poster child.

And I'm a two-time loser, Cate grumbled to herself. Nothing ever works out for me.

Cate reclined back, imagining Hunter's long eyelashes and emerald, green eyes. And that won't either! She shoved the pills in her mouth and took a long swig. For now, she would just snuggle with Smokey.

Hunter's fiery and itchy crotch demanded his attention immediately. He could barely hold himself up against the wall to urinate. I need to find that cream the doctor prescribed. Hunter's medicine cabinet was full between t-shots bottles and needles; he didn't have much room. Band aids, razors, and his toothbrush all fell into the sink.

"God dammit!" Hunter screamed. "What is wrong with me?!"

Some of Susie's old medicine's bottles were on the top shelf. Hunter located his cream on the back of the toilet, pulled down his pajamas and sighed with immediate relief. His unsteady and sweaty hands indicated he needed his T-shot immediately. For a split second, he considered taking one of Suzie's stronger pain pills but instead he tossed all her bottles in the trash and placed his tablets and the cream on the top shelf. Those pills mess my head up anyway.

His upper thigh was like his grandmother's pin cushion, a trail of little pricks from the T. Hunter had overcome his fear of needles when Stan would secretly stash his dope and syringes on Lisa's bookshelf right next to her favorite read The Outsiders by S.E Hinton. Stan knew she would find it, hoped she would experiment. It would make her feel at ease. But instead, it backfired. Lisa got used to seeing needles, even had a healthy respect for them, but she became oblivious to the contents of what was in the kite-folded envelope. She never wanted any part of it.

Stan never gives up, though. He teased and belittled Lisa incessantly. If he couldn't get her quiet with drugs, he found other ways.

"Fucking Outsiders.... You're a freak, Lisa. You will never be Dallas - he is a man. Besides I'm Dallas, just like him, tough, and the ladies love me." Stan schlepped his greasy cigarette from behind his ear and lit it.

"When I grow up, I'm going to write a book and I can be anyone I choose to be." Lisa jabbed back.

"Well, it won't be like The Outsiders. Men are better writers than women. You're no S.E. Hinton." Stan scoffed, throwing Lisa's book down on the bed.

Lisa picked her book up and snickered. "S.E Hinton is a woman."

Hunter laughed. "Moron." The older Lisa got, the less Stan's insults hurt, and the smarter she became.

Hunter gave himself his shot, and stretched, admiring himself in the full-length bathroom mirror. He slowly stripped his shirt and underwear off, posing to show off his defined abs and muscular chest. He playfully followed his body hair down with a finger, a large patch on his pecs with a line that traveled down his torso and blended in with his pelvic bone. An impish grin spread across his lips while he delicately held his penis. It's not perfect but it's mine.

He slicked his hair back into a duck tail like his father's with his black Fonz comb. I'm finally home.

By the next afternoon, Cate did not know what to do with herself. She had always worked; her career was all she had left, now. She wanted to call Michael, but had no strength left to stand up to his disdain. As Cate added cream and sugar to her coffee, she wondered if she was as selfish and self-serving as Michael and her ex always said. Her addiction had certainly cost Cate her marriage and her son. But she was weary of everyone passing judgment on her. Donna, her ex, her son, and her co-workers. No one knew, much less assessed, what it had been like living in her skin. Except Hunter.

She really clamored for a friend. That old familiar sentiment of wanting to get high flooded her and sent her spinning like a top.

"I wish Hunter was here!" She could not evade this indifference of despair and loneliness. As she went through her cupboards looking for her last hidden stash, she aimed to push out of her mind how Michael would cry as a toddler, trying to wake her up from her drug-induced stupor. He was just hungry. And then, just like that, the guilt and heartbreak set in, pinning her under fast like the current in a river.

Hunter sat in front of his computer, trying to vanish into the lyrics of his favorite CD, almost like some sort of astral projection. But the hard chair put too much pressure on his sore constituent. Trying to get used to his new physical accessory would be challenging, but he knew how long he had suffered to obtain this purification. He would find his way back to the memoir. I need to.

At first Hunter had written to sanitize himself from all the toxins and negativity in his life. Stan, Jimmie, even Sara. Then one day it hit him he didn't want to cleanse himself, he wanted to transform.

Hunter fidgeted. "These stupid bandages!" Oh, how he wanted to see Cate. Not just because she was so good at her work. Cate piqued his curiosity. As he played with the piece of paper that had Cate's number on it, Hunter tried to talk himself out of calling her. "I don't need to get involved with someone. I need to work on me."

This logic was not helping him with his restlessness. Hunter's batteries were low. "Maybe the night air will help."

Cate stomped through the trashed kitchen, clattering the dishes in the China cabinet. She didn't want to go any further down the tube. She dumped all her reminding pills down the toilet. Smokey joined her, watching them whirl around until they disappeared down into the hollow tunnel.

She snagged her coat, stepped outside. It was a chilly evening; she could see her breath puff out and then disappear toward the sky. Cate's head began to pound like a jackhammer. Withdrawal, so fast. Her distorted vison ballooned her head, almost as if her head was searching for her body. She counted the lines on each sidewalk to distract herself, playfully stopping to jump on a hopscotch game, pink chalk, and sneaker scuffs. The night air cleared her head and for a moment her body reconnected.

Hunter recovered his coat and headed out. Walking helped with writing.

Susie's things in the house distracted him too much. "That woman should come get her stuff. I told her months ago." Hunter clamped his teeth together.

As he hiked down the street the weight and soreness at his core made it hard to concentrate, but he forced himself to think about the chapter he wanted to finish – a portrait of his parents. His mom said he was a mirror image of his father. They were both so gentle, loved animals and nature. As Hunter/Lisa grew up, his beautiful and mentally ill mother seeped through his veins and shaped him, too. Of course, toxic memories of Stan intruded — no matter how hard he tried to escape him, Stan was there in his walk, hair, and most of all his scent. Life really was contradictory. The things we run from are embedded in us, forever branded in our psyche. I'm not Stan and I never will be. He picked up the pace.

Cate wandered, lost in her thoughts, open and raw. In the distance, she caught a glimpse of someone or something coming near her, moving with a cocky walk. She contemplated crossing over to the other side of the street. As the darkness slowly began to rest, the outline of the man came to light.

"Cate? Is that you?" Hunter was already aware of the answer, but it was necessary to say it out loud. Automatically, she put on her armor — her eyes seemed to harden, and her cheekbones tightened. Her painted fingernails curved like daggers or claws. It took a minute for her to loosen up.

"I knew it was you. You walk in such long strides. Were you a model? I always thought you must have been before you became a nurse." He examined Cate, admired her collar bone above her blouse. A heart-shaped necklace dangled over her jacket. Cate was a natural beauty.

"Hunter, I'm so glad to see you! How are things going?" Cate's insides were twisting. Being around Hunter outside of the hospital was magical. She could not help but admire him. His voice deep and husky, he had full facial hair, and his well-defined jawline very noticeable. She knew he was a man inside and out.

"Cate, would you like to go somewhere and talk? There's a coffee shop on the corner."

She recognized that she should not go but she answered without thinking. "Yes."

As they strolled together, an effortless vibe anchored in between them. Their gazes locked a little longer as they unfastened.

Still, Hunter surmised Cate was protecting a dark secret she hoped he wouldn't discover. The sadness pooling in her eyes created a barrier, and she hesitated before speaking too many times. Hunter deciphered that he could help her. It was critical to gain her trust.

In the coffee shop, they were suddenly anonymous. They were invisible. And together.

Hunter chatted strategically. Cate was an intricate puzzle just waiting for someone to support her, find her lost piece, delicate behind her tough exterior. She exuded such strength but behind her veil was a scared, vulnerable little girl. Hunter wanted to be gentle. Cate's trust awaited.

Across the table, Cate was measuring Hunter up. She could tell the way he sat he was not all the way healed up. Part of her did not want to play this game of getting to know each other. She suspected it would go nowhere. Another part of her wanted to disclose everything. His bright green eyes danced as he fixated upon her. She studied a picture on the wall and imagined running barefoot through the woods, freeing herself from her own captivity.

"How are things going at work?" Hunter hated his vague question, but he preferred to go slow. Start with something safe.

Cate narrowed her almond shaped eyes, flattened of depth and emotion. "Work is going OK, I guess. But I really want to know how you're healing up." Cate hated lying about work, but it was too complicated.

"I have my moments. It is hard to change my bandages on my own. Maybe you could give me some tips." Hunter belly laughed. Am I really flirting with her? Go slow Hunter. Cate's long blonde hair shone in the shop's lights, giving the appearance of a spark in her eyes. He was entranced. But he proceeded with caution. Cate appeared a little hard, harder than he recollected.

"Is there anyone at home to help you?" Cate spoke with anticipation in her voice.

"No, there isn't." Hunter blew on his hot coffee.

"I'm sorry, I don't mean to pry. I figured you would have someone at home."

Hunter could sense her curiosity. "Susie – my girlfriend — left when I started to transition. She wanted to be with a woman. I can't blame her for knowing what she wanted." Hunter visualized himself diving into Cate's stormy eyes, floating in a blue lagoon, waiting for her to swim across to capture him.

"You're too forgiving. She must have known who you were deep down. I mean, you emit male energy."

Hunter wasn't really paying attention to her words; he studied her energy. Cate's long nails circling her coffee cup with pent-up power, sexuality that was contained and present at the same time. Hunter wanted to unwrap Cate layer by layer and worship every part of her.

"Excuse me, I need to use the powder room."

Cate skated away with the skill of a ballerina leaving him wanting. A rush of desire rolled through him. A new wave of confidence percolated through his veins.

"Where is my fucking compact?" In the bathroom, Cate ransacked her purse to find the makeup, and was stunned at her nervousness.

But he was so compelling! His eyes were a dark green with yellow flecks swirling around like caramel candy. He strutted like a cowboy walking into a saloon after riding his horse in the desert for days. Hunter's energy lured you in completely, his natural ability to understand someone who was struggling opened a window to his compassion. Why was she denying herself?

At the table, Cate scanned Hunter's big, soft hands as they stirred sugar into his coffee. They seemed paradoxical, something new and intoxicating. When he excused himself, she had a moment to marvel at his beauty. His muscular thighs outlined against his jeans. His smell, gaze, and body left her head spinning. This is my chance! Cate repeated to herself, to be happy, and I'm going to take it! She became like a starved lion ready to pounce on unexpected prey.

The men's room is always on the left. Hunter grunted – he had automatically rotated to the right and bumped into an old woman coming out of the ladies' restroom. The old woman's face told the same old story. Shock and disgust spread throughout her body, reminding him of Stan, and a hundred other people who had gawked at Lisa like a freak.

"Why are you stealing my shirts? What the fuck is wrong with you?" Stan yelled, showing off his silver tooth. "I don't know what is going on with you, but what I do know is you're a fucking birth defect!"

Stan had slammed his fist on the coffee table, sending his stupid reindeer cup bouncing, then exploding into bits and pieces on the floor. Part of Lisa giggled knowing that was his favorite cup. Stan hated when he didn't have control over her, or any woman, for that matter.

Lisa/Hunter hated him, an old hate that was a volcano waiting to erupt. When Hunter became older, he would realize Stan despised himself and it didn't have anything to do with him. When he finally comprehended Stan's hatred for himself, he knew his own power. That's when Hunter's strength started to blossom. Stan's friends stopped coming around because he had cornered them in a room and threatened them. Lisa had to constantly shoot down his perverted advances, worse than the constant bullying at school, and exhausting. Sometimes Lisa envisioned stabbing him in the neck. Now that he was complete, Hunter still planned his revenge up close and personal, the same as Stan. He sucked down his rage and washed his hands.

His thoughts were interrupted by Cate, looking quietly out the window, still as a portrait, stunning. It snapped him back. Hunter longed to ask her to come home with him. The words were stuck in his throat and vanished into the air, never to be spoken, as he sank back into his seat with a groan and a nod.

Cate adjusted her clothes as she rose from the table. She needed to center herself. She ought to get home.

"I'm so happy we ran into each other, but I have to run." Cate shielded her eyes from him, trying to hide the defeat. She knew well enough the pattern her life always took. Cate was drawn into pain like a moth to light, and the worst pain came from failing over and over with people. Is Hunter worth the inevitable disappointment waiting in the shadows? Could it be different? Cate toyed with the notion, then dismissed the idea.

You don't need to be frightened of me but if you want to leave, I understand," he said quietly.

Hunter recognized Cate's indecision and fear. He wanted to stop her, swoop in with pinpoint accuracy and precision. Cate was exposed like prey, and he was the eagle. It unnerved her, enclosed like a black funnel cloud throwing her into the fear of being torn apart and cast into a million shards of glass.

Her eyes began to turn a stormy grey as she scrambled to drape her coat over her strong shoulders, and shapely back. Hunter couldn't overcome the frost forming in his veins.

"Hunter, I'm leaving now. I hope to see you soon. By the way - I'm not frightened I'm just careful."

Before he could respond she sailed away. Hunter loved a challenge and Cate offered one. He couldn't resist her. All he could do was wait and see, until their paths crossed again.

I want to unwrap you Cate. Hunter savored the last drops of his coffee, getting ready for the hike back to his empty house.

CHAPTER 4

Cate caught a glimpse of herself in a furniture store window. Her necklace sparkled in the streetlight. She rested against the glass, steadying herself.

The sidewalk was rushing up in waves. Was she going to throw up? She always ended up in this situation. Hunter was trying to reach out to her and what did she do? Run for cover. She sat down on a bus bench. The old, wicked storm rose, and she hid her head in her hands. Why would he want me? My own parents didn't want me. Michael doesn't want me. I have nothing.

She was forced into memory, helpless, sitting on the cold hard wooden pew outside the Department of Human Services. These offices were her only stable home environment, such as they were. Everywhere else became temporary, but not the wooden pews, they became her sanctuary, even a confessional. It's no use. That's the way it is, she concluded. I'm a nurse. I can help people. I helped him. That's all there is now.

Hunter placed his money under the saucer, a heaviness filling his chest. As he left the café, he blocked Cate from his mind and tried to focus on what he needed to do. He was running out of money from his last writing gig. He had to come up with some fresh story ideas, but he wasn't inspired now.

He passed a homeless man. What was his story? A shiny cup dived out to him, desperate for change. Hunter examined his face, the sunken cheekbones under dirty and matted hair. That light burnt out long ago. Hunter tossed four coins in his cup, noting the clanking sound as the money dropped.

That sound drove him back. When Lisa dropped to her knees to suck off the neighborhood boys, change always fell out of her pockets. Girl's clothes. Useless. He didn't have to wear those now.

"You don't need to rush off, Lisa." Larry smirked as he buttoned his jeans. "We could hang out." Larry was a nice guy, but Sara is the one that I want.

"I'm going to the arcade." Lisa said over her shoulder as she gathered up the coins she had stole from Stan when he was passed out.

"Sara is too busy with her new boyfriend. She doesn't hang out there anymore."

"Shut up Larry!" Lisa hated when he was right.

† † †

Back at home, Cate collapsed into her nightclothes and slippers, and went looking for Smokey. As usual, he was inside the bedroom closet, cocooned in the old clothes piled on the floor.

"Still pining after him, Smokey?" Cate raised her eyebrow. "Give it up."

I should have given Hunter a chance tonight. Cate was tired of that little girl sitting on the wooden bench waiting for someone to want her. She had fought hard to find her place in this world. Tomorrow she would call Michael whether he wanted to talk or not.

† † †

Hunter found his drink and stretched out on the sofa. Cate's number on the coffee table teased him. Her beautiful cursive, flowing, wild, and with a hint of danger. The perfect combination.

Did I say something wrong? Hunter mused. He took the T from the table. The sharp jab from the needle jolted him back. These damn testosterone shots!

The aching sensation in his groin wouldn't subside. Thinking about Cate made it worse. How he longed to use his new addition. He was a tangled ball of wire messy and imprecise. He wanted a beautiful release to flow through him and heal him. He could recite his therapist's words by heart. "What are you running to?" Not what are you running from. That was the million-dollar question. It was unrealistic to want Cate to fill his emptiness. That task had his name on it.

But imagining Cate's curves, a surge of excitement pulsed through him. Hunter imagined he had an orgasm. Her body teased him to touch and overpower her. It would appease him to have Cate submit, her long, sword-like fingernails scratching up his back...

Hunter had travelled these dangerous waters before. He was aware of what treachery could do. Sara and Jimmie smashed his nose in it. Their betrayal devastated him. Stan's failed in comparison. It had been almost a sacred experience. Lisa had cornered Sara to try and explained what happened but instead Sara refused to talk to her. Cate had done the same thing – no she hadn't. But it hurt the same. Just as he began to ease into his fantasy, he tightened up – was he becoming like Stan? A predator?

Heat filled his head, radiated through his extremities, a cleansing of his body and soul. Yes, Hunter was like his brother, a man, but the difference was he didn't want to annihilate Cate – he didn't want her to take his pain. Hunter closed his eyes.

Cate avoided looking at her phone. She was afraid to call Michael, torn. He never got over the divorce and the "deceit." That's what he called it.

"Get the fuck over it!" Cate shrieked at the phone. Smokey galloped across the room and hid in the closet. Then, summoning her courage, she selected her son's name in her contact list.

"Hello, Michael."

He hesitated. "What do you want? I told you not to contact me!"

Cate took a deep breath. "You're not the only one who suffered from the divorce. Quite frankly, you're not the only person to suffer in this world!"

"How dare you try to even act like you can quantify my pain and suffering. At least I know who I am!" The line went dead.

Cate's anger and fury ran through her bones. "Spoiled brat! I know who I am!" She picked up his photo and smashed it against the wall.

Cate ached for a pill. She couldn't escape them — Michael, Donna, her ex, and of course her parents. Well, her foster parents who received a check every month. At least she had a bed to sleep in and food to eat. But they all insisted she cover up who she really was, her "quirks." Everyone wanted Cate to "blend in." Their shame was written all over their faces. They were inadequate parents because they couldn't fix her. That's what they thought anyway. It's all bullshit!

Cate realized she needed to speak with Hunter and apologize for her abrupt exit, but she didn't have his number. Maybe he would contact her. She buried herself in a book to lose herself for a while.

Hunter was awakened by the woodpecker drilling into a tree outside his window. He had a little too much to drink last night and his mouth was dry as bone. He spilled water on the floor trying to fill the coffee pot up but ignored it.

Sitting on the deck with his morning coffee, Hunter admired the billowy clouds. They reminded him of Cate in her clean white uniform and how it shaped her thick body, almost cupping it. But then he reminded himself; she wasn't interested. Hunter flipped his hands palm up prompting a disturbing memory of Stan.

"Mom is in the hospital for a while so that means I'm the boss." Stan spread a white powder on the table, rolled up a dollar bill and inhaled the glistening powder up his nose. "Here, I saved one for you."

"No, I'm good." Lisa had to get as far away as she could. As she headed for the front door, he lunged at her and dragged her back.

"Where the fuck you think you're going?" Stan growled and stood in the doorway.

"Anywhere but here." Lisa rolled her eyes and rammed Stan out of her way.

"Listen here, you little bitch! You think your hot shit? You don't need me anymore? I know about you and Larry. He told me. Messing around with him — it won't get you anywhere near Sara, freak! She doesn't want you, Lisa! You don't have the right equipment!" Stan corralled his penis suggestively.

"I never needed you! If you don't leave me alone, I'll tell EVERYONE your twisted, sick secrets!" Lisa clenched her teeth so hard she checked with her fingers to make sure she hadn't chipped a tooth! As she ran down the hill to her favorite oak tree, Lisa had an epiphany.

"Stan can't poison me anymore. I am stronger than he is. I am reborn. Hunter will be my new name – my Indian name." Lisa used her pocketknife to dig the new name into the tree. "I'm free."

Lisa's – now Hunter's — father was part Native American. He would say, "When you consume an animal's spirit you honor the beautiful creature by using every piece of them. They gave their life so you can sustain nourishment. Their fur warms you from the bitter cold. And their bones are tools to use in battle and unearth the soil for planting."

Hunter's father was a proud, gentle man. He would tell his child about the Indian's understanding of being "Two-Spirited," a welcome and important person in the tribe. It was the white man's fear and ignorance that distorted what it meant to be two-spirited. Like Hunter was.

"You have both masculine and feminine spirit in you." Hunter's father told him. Now Lisa knew she could be Hunter. A true two-spirit.

Hunter headed back to the house with a new sense of empowerment. Stan was insignificant now. Hunter went home and stood in the doorway, unafraid.

"I knew that you wouldn't go far. Now sit by me and drink a beer." Stan patted the seat cushion next to him. Hunter sat down next to him. It made him laugh a little, that Stan still saw Lisa.

Stan's hands found his way to Lisa's arm. "You owe me one Lisa. The last time, we were interrupted." Stan's smiled his stupid and crooked smile.

Hunter flipped his knife out and strategically placed it on Stan's groin. "My name is Hunter now. If you ever touch me again, I will cut your cock off, you sick and twisted fuck!"

That was the last time Stan tried anything. It was a good memory. A mourning dove landed on the fencepost, singing his delightful but tragic song. Hunter finished his coffee and made a quick decision. He had some unresolved issues to address with Susie before he could pursue Cate.

Hunter went inside to change his clothes, rehearsing the conversation with Susie. Did he just need to show her that he weathered the storm, and he didn't need her anymore? Was he just being vindictive? Part of him wanted to make her suffer and doubt herself just like she always did to him. At the same time, he knew that Susie didn't plant the seed of self-doubt in Hunter. That went back to the incest. And when Lisa realized she would never be a boy.

Visiting her dad for the weekend was a breath of fresh air. On this weekend Lisa, her sister, and her sister's best friend, Claire, were going to the amusement park. Lisa's jealously engulfed her as Claire's boyfriend showed up unexpectedly, interrupting Lisa's fantasy that she was her boyfriend. Lisa sat between them, keeping her boyfriend at arm's length. She wanted to feel Claire press up against her arm when the ride spun and tossed them around. But Claire snuggled close to the boy instead. Tears began to stream down Lisa's face. Hiding behind a big oak tree, Lisa dropped to her knees and looked up to the sky for answers.

"God, please make me a boy so I'll be loved! I hate my body! I don't want to be a girl!"

Hunter reminded himself he was finally complete. He could make things happen. As he gathered his car keys, he said to himself, "She will see. She will see." Once Susie was in the past, his future would be full of opportunity.

Michael's phone call left Cate numb. She picked up her phone and tossed it onto her pile of unpaid bills. Work was going to call, she knew it. Fate wasn't in her favor. Her life kept spinning out of control, vaporizing, and vanishing into space, erasing her existence. To make matters worse, her ex had been texting her and wanted to meet up and talk about Michael. Cate ignored the texts. Enough was enough.

Cate slammed her drink back and crunched on the ice cubes sending a rush of metallic pain throughout her jaw. The liquor spread like a map and left her lightheaded. Even Smokey was leery of the tension in the room as he circled around the front window. Something was up.

The doorbell rang and Cate stood very still. She hadn't had visitors for some time. Smokey darted past her and clawed at the front door. Cate knew who it was before she opened the door and saw the woman waiting, lighting a cigarette flirtatiously.

"Hello Edward. You clean up well. You should - with all the money you spent. But you're still playing dress up."

Cate could hear the contempt in her voice. She shouldn't be short with her ex-wife; she was stunning as always. Her dark curly hair fell down her back in feathery strands, her cherry red lipstick and dark makeup suggested a night out on the town.

"What can I help you with, Gwen?"

You know, at first when you would wear my panties and bra's I didn't mind. It was our little secret. You stretched out my expensive lingerie, but remember? I was a good sport. We played well together for a while. And now you don't even answer my texts, Edward!" Gwen spoke with malice in her voice as she shoved her way inside. "Well, hello, my darling Smokey. I hope you're happy to see me!"

Cate's eyes narrowed. "I've asked you not to call me by my birth name. It's Cate now."

"How could I forget your big announcement. The beginning of the end to our marriage." Gwen exhaled through her nostrils, almost admitting defeat. "Is that my blouse? Really Edward we have been through this your shoulder are too broad. May I smoke inside?"

"If you must. Why are you here? I know you're still polluting Michael's mind with stories of my supposed deceit. And by the way, this blouse matches my complexion. It always washed you out." Cate knew she was being mean but didn't care.

"Of your supposed deceit? Edward it was a betrayal!" Gwen tugged hard on her cigarette. "Can you really blame him? One minute he has a normal family, a mother and father. Then the next moment his world is turned upside down with two mothers divorced, and no home life. Besides, you never considered what it would do to me. I married Edward, not Cate. You were selfish!" Gwen smashed her cigarette out in the ugly ashtray that "Edward," had purchased for her in Mexico.

Cate had always hated that ashtray. "Did you even consider how I might be affected when I came home to find you in bed with the neighbor? Everyone knew but me. I was the laughingstock of the whole neighborhood!" Cate flung her arms out helplessly.

"I have needs, too." Gwen lit another cigarette.

"Will you quit smoking like a truck driver? It took me weeks to get the nicotine smell out of the carpet and bedding," Cate barked.

"Listen, Edward, you have a lot of nerve! I covered up to everyone about your drinking and drugs. Until you left Michael to drown in the bathtub, that is. You were supposed to be watching him!" Gwen voiced cracked with emotion.

"Gwen." Cate had to sit down. "I can't escape that day. It never goes away."

"What about Michael? I'm sure it haunts him too. He called me today. It took an hour to calm him down. Don't call him anymore, Edward. He isn't ready to talk to you, and the truth is I don't know if he ever will be."

"We have been through this a million times, Gwen! It was never my intention to hurt or mislead either of you. This is who I have always been, and I'll not apologize anymore." Cate saw the color drain out of her ex-wife's face.

Edward did love Gwen, once. But when he was finally able to shed his skin of secrets and concealment, a rebirthing process was set in motion. Now Edward was dead; now she was Cate. Cate still loved Michael but didn't love Gwen.

"Ed... Sorry. Cate, I won't take up any more of your time. You said in your text that you found my mother's earrings?"

"That was three weeks ago. But — Yes, I'll get them." To her dismay. Gwen followed her into the bedroom.

As Cate opened the closet, Smokey flew in and circled the men's suits and ties in the cardboard box.

"Apparently, Smokey misses Edward, too. I thought you had already given those suits to charity."

It was a weird situation, but she wanted to give them to Michael. They were beautiful, designer suits. But Michael wasn't ready to accept Cate or such an intimate gift.

Cate lobbed the box at Gwen. "I had the earrings cleaned for you. I figured it was the least I could do. And yes, I did steal some of your clothes. And I kept Edward's old suits because I wanted Michael to have them. It's how he remembers me. This is how he sees me. Will you take them, too?"

She accepted the bundle. "I'll have to have them cleaned. But — I can give the suits to Michael. It might soften the blow. They're beautiful suits. He looks just like you – did. Edward, I mean, Cate this is it. Leave him be. I'll show myself out."

Cate closed the closet door.

Gwen suddenly seemed gentle, and said quietly, "You and Michael are more alike than you both will admit. Take care."

Cate stood motionless in the doorway as she vanished.

> *But never have been a blue calm sea.*
> *I have always been a storm. Always been a storm.*

Fleetwood Mac's mystical lyrics plunged out of Cate's mouth. Gwen had always been a storm. In the beginning, it drew them together. But now the chaos and pandemonium were waning. The storm was passing.

As he drove, Hunter built up his courage to talk with Susie. Things between them ended abruptly. But what did he want to ask? What should he say? When Hunter was younger, He thought every situation in life was a puzzle and we were sent out into the world to find the pieces so they would fit perfectly into place. A skeleton key to open a door filled with certainty, lost treasure. He was still eager to finish every puzzle, an unquenchable longing for closure that became Hunter's unconscious drive and ambition.

When he looked like Lisa, he had to use other people for this task. Larry. Maybe Susie. The hollowness picked at him. But becoming Hunter meant starting to understand his uniqueness. His complexity. The true power was integrating Lisa and Hunter. They were interconnected. No one could fill up his hollowness but him. First, he had to close the loop with Susie.

On the gravel road to Susie's house, the frost leaves were a broken trail leading Hunter to the unknown. As he drove closer he saw the trees coiling the old house like a snake. It looked foreign suddenly. Funny how some places used to make you seem so secure and safe, just to become empty shells, meaningless. Hunter drove into the driveway and parked, gathering his racing thoughts. As he approached the front door his hand rested on his chest, Hunter had arrived.

"You still have your swagger, that's for sure." Susie exhaled loudly, while unlocking the screen door.

"I see that you're still dropping your shoulder. Didn't Coach Adams teach you anything?" Hunter jabbed at her confidence.

"Still a smart ass, too. So, Lisa, what brings you around here? Chasing demons or trying to settle the score?"

"It's Hunter, not Lisa. Anyway, I have some of your stuff." Hunter placed the box on the porch.

"Why do you feel the need to rub my nose in it?" Susie scoffed.

"Is that what you really think?" Hunter's voice raised a bar as his green eyes changed to blue.

Susie gave him a sideways look. "Or maybe you want to come back? Lisa, I told you how I felt about this whole transgender business. I wanted to be with a woman. I'm not straight!"

"Susie, you can't tell me you had no idea what direction I was going."

"I knew you were very masculine, and I could deal with it. When I realized it was more than just flannel shirts and boxer briefs, I, well... panicked. I don't think you understand how hard all of this has been on me. It's not all about you—my life was also affected. I wanted you to be my life partner."

"I'm sorry, Susie... I really wanted us to work. But if you were really into me like you say you were, how could you not have known?"

"It doesn't really matter if I knew or not. The point is — it's not what I signed up for." Susie made no move to invite him in, her arms crossed as she pressed against the door jam.

Hunter could not control his tongue. "What I didn't sign up for was you walking out on me. We had plans, Susie, don't you remember? We wanted to get married and have children."

"So that's it? You're disappointed. How predictable!" Susie shouted.

"Predictable? I will tell you what is predictable. Daddy's little rich girl who gets what she needs, and if someone doesn't fit in to your perfect little picture, then they're swept under the table. I mean, come on Susie, you're 39 and your parents don't know about your sexual preference! I loved you. I wish you would've known that." Hunter circled back to his car. This was not what he had planned, and he could kick himself that he had fallen back into the old argument.

"Wait Hunter... look I'm sorry I don't want to fight." Susie inched closer. "Let me try again. Why don't you come inside and have a drink? We can talk. Maybe I was wrong. I must say you look fine in your Levi's." Susie batted her eyes and squeezed Hunter's shoulder.

"No, Susie." Hunter removed her hands. "You don't get what you want."

"You are a selfish asshole, Lisa. Yeah, I said Lisa!"

All the bluster drained out of him. Susie had to do this alone. He turned away, opened his truck door, and prepared himself for the lonely drive home.

Remorse was beginning to set in now. Hunter had wanted to hurt her, and he had succeeded. Was he that much of an asshole? A familiar song was playing on the radio. I'm not in love... but I'm open to persuasion. He fingered Cate's number on the torn-out piece of paper in his pocket. He pulled over to make that call, his shaking fingers fumbling to find the digits.

"Hello," Cate's voice rang out clear and concise.

Hunter stiffened for a moment, caught off guard by her husky and angelic voice. "Cate, hello. It's Hunter. I've been thinking about you. I wanted to come over and talk." Hunter spoke with a confidence he didn't really feel.

"I'd love that... I could use a friend right now. I will text you, my address."

Hunter drove to Cate's house with anticipation and excitement. The air was clean and crisp, holding within it a lure of hope and change. His demons were quiet, and Hunter could ignore them for a little while.

Turning into Cate's driveway, Hunter saw a beautiful cream-colored cat in the window. It reminded him of Snowflake. His cat had been his sanctuary from all the chaos at home. Hunter adjusted himself in the car mirror. He ran his fingers through his thick dark hair and unbuttoned the top button of his shirt. Beads of sweat were forming on Hunter's back and slowly traveling down to soak up in his underwear band. As he walked up the driveway the curtain slid open and shut.

Cate answered the door wearing a very revealing silk dress, her breasts accentuated. "Hunter, you look well, it's wonderful to see you. Please come in."

Hunter followed her in and couldn't help but to be entranced by her erotic scent. For all his fantasy of being an eagle at the coffee shop, he suddenly discovered maybe he was being summoned to his own slaughter. Cate was a black widow, her home her web, and he was the unassuming victim. Hunter couldn't take his eyes off her.

"Would you like a drink?" Cate's voice was raspy and had a bluesy sound to it. She poured scotch in two glasses.

Cate's stare was intense and a little intimating. Her eyes were slowly undressing him, and his pulse was sending electricity to his groin. Her seductive dress was not an accident. Hunter wanted to savor this moment.

"So why did you decide to call me? I'm glad you did." Cate's words slowly brushed against her lips as she pounded back her scotch.

Hunter met her gaze. "Many reasons. I wanted to thank you for your exceptional care at the hospital. I know it's your job, but you went above and beyond the call of duty."

Cate found her way toward him, her dress floating across the floor creating the illusion of water flowing. She sat down beside him.

"You're correct. I was doing my job, but I had another motive." Cate flushed and averted her big, revealing eyes.

"What motive would that be?" Some part of Hunter already knew, but he wanted to hear it from Cate's mouth.

"I think we both know what that is." Cate glanced away.

Cate poured them both another scotch. The color in her eyes changed as she shot back the brown liquid. Her assurance kicked in and washed over her. Hunter's lust created tunnel vision. His hands start to roam, finding their way to Cate's exposed thighs. He pressed his mouth against her ruby red lips, tasting them, circling his tongue to find hers. A deep primitive hunger arose from inside him. He leaned into Cate, spreading her legs open as he placed his aching body on top of her.

Cate was taken by surprise from her desire; it had been a long time since she was with anyone. Gwen had to have been the last time and she had been Edward, then. Cate cringed at the thought. She had never experienced sex as Cate. The last time she tried was with a man she met on a dating site. Cate had made her status clear in her profile, but her first date was a psychopath who loved trans women but only pre surgery. It's the best of both worlds. Cate shuddered. When Cate told him she had bottom surgery and that her profile clearly mentioned it, she had said, innocently, if you're gay I can introduce you to some of my friends.

"You fucking bitch!" He smacked Cate hard cutting her upper lip. "I'm not gay. I will show you gay slut!"

Hunter saw her pull back. "Cate where are you?"

"Right here with you."

Her hands wandered through Hunter's thick hair, stroked his well-formed biceps. Hunter's scent was strong and musky, sending Cate swooning and begging to taste him. Hunter's manhood was against her, rubbing slowly.

Hunter took his shirt off and Cate kissed his scars, running her fingers delicately across them. Her breath was hot against his face her big eyes rolled back into her head. Hunter reached around her strong, full back and unsnapped her bra. Cate's vulnerability made Hunter feel both powerful, and somehow vulnerable, too.

Cate was finding it extremely difficult to concentrate. She didn't know how to tell Hunter the truth, but she had to. She wasn't afraid of rejection, but he had to be prepared – what if there was a problem? The last guy – he had tried to force her. She never found out what would have happened – she shouted for help, escaped. Hunter was a sexy man, but was she ready? Would she be all right? She ignored her inner voice and continued to explore his body thoroughly.

This magnificent creature, she thought to herself. She slid down onto her knees and ran her hands up his hairy legs, admiring his rock-hard calves. She understood from her own experience and research that his penis wouldn't operate correctly yet. But it was still hot touching him through his tight underwear. He was breathing hard as she stroked him gently.

Hunter was on the verge of having an orgasm but knew that he couldn't really finish all the way. He pushed Cate back onto her back and placed his fingers on her inner thighs again. As he slowly began to massage her, Cate snatched his hand away in a panic.

"I'm sorry, I can't! I want to, but I can't!" Cate got up and seized the bottle, poured another drink.

"Why? We have a connection. The chemistry is undeniable."

"Yes, of course, but… I'm not really who you think I am." Cate aimlessly played with her necklace.

"What, you were an FBI agent or a spy from another country." Hunter laughed out loud. "All I view is a beautiful, intelligent young woman. A woman I want to know better." Hunter's deep dimples were irresistible.

"What if I told you that I spent a lot of money on my appearance?" Cate looked away.

"Many women have cosmetic surgery, Cate. Listen, there isn't anything you can say to scare me away." Hunter lightly brushes Cate's hair out of her sky-blue eyes. "Besides, I already know." Hunter poured himself another drink.

"You do?" Cate was stunned. "I mean, what do you think you know?"

"That scar on your inner leg. I know what that is. Also, when you bent over to pour my drink, I saw the scars on your chest and the make-up to conceal it. You had reassignment surgery."

"So, you knew this whole time?"

"I was waiting for you to be comfortable enough to tell me."

"Are you OK with it?" Cate sat down.

"Why wouldn't I be? Look, I didn't want to pressure you to tell your story. Tell me when you're ready."

"Thank you, Hunter. So, if you want to ask me questions you can. I don't talk about my life much."

Hunter cupped her soft hands in his. "Well... let me think... What was your birth name?" He gently stroked the long veins in her fingers.

"Edward. Edward started transitioning over ten years ago. His family disowned him. Michael - his son - despises him and so does his ex-wife, Gwen. She ruined his life. He lost everything—job, house, son. He had to change careers. Then, he – I — became a nurse. But Edward's depression was spinning out of control. He totally isolated himself.

"How did you – he – get out of it?"

"His therapists dished out anti-depressants like candy." Cate paused and drank her scotch. "Edward also — he self-medicated with opiates. But he was caught stealing from work, and eventually, was caught and went to rehab. It's still – when we first met, Edward – I — messed up again. So, there you have it." Cate glanced down at the floor and waited a few moments. "Well, aren't you going to say something?" Cate blurted out.

Hunter chuckled. "I don't scare that easy. It sounds hard. I always knew we had a connection...now I know why." Hunter needed to approach this lightly.

"Cate, if you don't mind me asking. Why do you refer to yourself in third person?"

"Edward was never a part of me. He was a thorn in my side. I'm erasing Edward. You must think I'm crazy." Cate finished her drink.

"On the contrary, I find you fascinating. Also, completely stunning."

Cate sat beside him, caressed his handsome face. "You're so good-looking, and a sweet man. You don't need to bring sex to the undesirable." Cate mischievously runs her fingers through his sexy goatee.

This exquisite beauty. There she is waiting for me to uncover her, to crack her shell wide open. Hunter's mind bouncing back and forth in this moment was exhilarating. Hunter set down his drink and bent forward into Cate.

"I know the world is against us, but I want to experience this moment with you right now." Hunter took her hands in his.

As Cate led him up the staircase, she imagined Hunter's hands all over her, teasing her, pulling her in, and finally helping her to connect the dots. But fear began to course through her body, too. She was expanding like a crab outgrowing its shell, but still trying to keep her hard, protective cover. "I'm not too sure what to do? I haven't been touched as Cate before."

Hunter embraced her back. His knees were shaky, and he leaned against the banister for a moment. Their connection had evolved into an emotional cocktail mixed with raw sensations and hidden agendas. Part of Hunter wanted to peel back the layers one by one.

"You're safe with me." There was so much power in letting go. Maybe they could start together.

Hunter's breath was crisp on her neck, sending jolts of electricity throughout her body. She turned to run her fingers across his lips, exploring the fresh wetness. His dark hair fell across her face as they landed together on her bed. He kissed her passionately. Cate's hands were all over his body, touching and searching his scars with beautifully put-together strokes filling in the puzzles. Cate fell deeper into Hunter's grasp with each stroke of his fingers. Her vision was blurred and all she could visualize were colors. They splashed against the wall melting together to form bright, scattered images.

The atmosphere was smoldering. Hunter stood to take his underwear off. Cate was in awe of him; he had no fear. It didn't matter to her that he couldn't use his new organ; their connection was so much more than that. He picked her up into his colossal arms and held her against his muscular chest. Hunter laid Cate across the brass bed, discovering her thoroughly with his fingers, lips, and tongue. Cate wrapped her long lean legs around his arched back. Their bodies dissolved in and out of each other.

As Hunter peered into Cate's eyes the walls began to disintegrate, and an unspoken trust began to surface. He bent his face slowly against hers, taking in all her natural beauty. His fingers and mouth were roaming about her chassis, finally settling between her legs. Cate nails clasped his hair as Hunter's fingers dissolved inside her. She gasped for air as her eyes spiraled back.

Cate moved him closer and let out a moaning scream, convulsing and shuddering. Hunter kissed her deep as she twisted up around him like a tree vine. Once the endless moment had passed, her hands searched lower to find him. The warmth and heat of her caress was invigorating, but he simply couldn't perform, much to his frustration. It was as if he was uncapable of opening, like a tight fist.

"It's not working right. You should know that." Hunter spoke with sarcasm.

Cate was trying to come back in her body. Elation surrounded her; she was beginning to relax deeply. Glancing at Hunter, she could almost see Lisa. They blended perfectly, as if he were two broken and jagged pieces of glass that created a completely beautiful and unique work of art. But Cate didn't know how to be truly intimate with another person, not as a woman. And seeing so clearly frightened her suddenly. Maybe Hunter could spot bits and pieces of Edward. To hide her turmoil, she collected her clothes.

"What's the hurry, Cate?" Hunter's green eyes danced in the light. Hunter lightly kissed the scar on Cate's thigh. Her memory flooded with that terrible night when her first "date" with a man, when she finally had the courage to join a dating service as a woman, he had cut her with a knife because she was fully female, fully herself. He would have killed her. Pervert. If she hadn't run, she would be dead.

Cate avoided eye contact. "This scar — a man tried to rape me. He stabbed me. You might want to put some clothes on. You'll catch cold." Cate's tone was suddenly icy.

"Cate, I would never hurt you. I'm not him! Do you think I'm like that?" Hunter spoke loudly. He was beginning to worry. She was falling back, and he wanted to pick her apart with hateful words, so she could experience his pain and vulnerability firsthand. The tricky part was that it never quite worked. If I say hateful things and hurt her then I'm no better than my brother. He got very quiet.

"No, Hunter that's not it. We just need to be realistic." Cate stepped behind the dresser to finish dressing.

"Realistic? What are you getting at?" Hunter's voice was almost a growl.

"How far do you really think this could go?" Cate's hands trembled as she instinctively touched her throat.

"I wasn't really thinking that far ahead." Hunter bit his lip and ran his fingers through his thick mane.

"Well, I have, and I've been doing this longer than you. We can't —" Cate snapped.

"Excuse me? I'VE BEEN DOING THIS MY WHOLE LIFE!" Hunter pounded his fist on the bedside table.

"You should go. I have things to do." Cate's voice was unsympathetic and cold.

Hunter could taste her fear, but at the same time he didn't want to beg for her attention. Hunter found his clothes. He stood, naked, visible, revealing himself to her with a smirk.

"I tell you what, Cate. Give me a call when you want something real." Hunter stomped away like a child that didn't get his way.

Cate landed onto the bed, wallowing in her self-pity, wishing the bottle of scotch wasn't still downstairs. What was wrong with her? She was still hungry for Hunter. Heading to the bathroom, she hoped a relaxing soak in the tub could help put her back together.

Hunter was modifying his clothing and trying to find his way to the front door when Smokey darted out in front him. "Sorry about all the yelling, big guy." Hunter knelt and stroked his thick fur.

Cate's walls were high as a mountain. The night air threatened snow and stabbed mercilessly into his lungs as he crept silently out the front door. Hunter was a fool. Lisa's old shame rose again, blending with this new disillusionment. Jimmie, Sara, now Cate. His eyes burned with tears.

He heard Sara's voice in his head. "Everyone knows what you're doing with my brother. It won't work you know. I'm not like you."

Lisa had tried to convince Sara, Hunter had tried to connect with Cate – but neither one wanted him, in the end.

CHAPTER 5

Hunter roared into the first bar he saw. It wasn't exactly the best neighborhood, but at this point he didn't care. Creature of habit he was, really. The negative energy hovered in the air, loud with the laughter of drunks, cheaters, and lost souls come to drown. Maybe she just wanted me to perform but I fucking can't!"

"What's your poison?" The bartender leaned towards Hunter.

Hunter saw the bartender's picket fence of missing teeth, took in his faded tattoos.

"Scotch on the rocks," Hunter hissed, void of any emotion.

Hunter craved the brown liquid that cushioned the ice cubes. It was something out of a turn-of-the-century movie. Classic with an element of tragedy.

Dark images sifted through his mind. Hunter shot back the brown liquid, trying not to choke on the bar's stench. Images of his encounter with Cate pierced his mind and sent bolts of lust and anxiety through his core. Out of the corner of his eye he saw a glint of blonde hair, and for a spilt second, he thought it was her. Had she followed him? He turned with a relieved grin.

"Hello, I'm Brandi, if you don't mind me joining you? You've a great smile! Buy me a drink?"

Her face was something off a magazine cover. He bit his lower lip and dragged his perfectly aligned teeth across his tongue.

"Sure, why not? What's your preference?"

"Vodka — let's do shots!" Her eyes were shining.

Hunter chuckled. "OK, make sure you can keep up!" He was having a hard time keeping his hunger from showing. Brandi's long, painted fingernails slowly circled the back of his hands as Hunter kept the shots flowing. Cate's scent was still on him, a dirty secret. Hell, he hadn't even showered yet.

"I forgot to mention - you look just like my ex-boyfriend." Brandi teased the buttons on Hunter's shirt.

"Really? He must be a good-looking guy." Hunter chuckled.

Brandi turned away and hammered her shot back. "Well, actually, he is a sadistic asshole!"

"Really?" Hunter angled closer as she hunched over the bar.

She rested into his shoulder. "I met him at a house party. A big strong bad boy with a swagger. I was hooked from the beginning." Brandi took a breath and lit a cigarette she had fished out of her oversized purse.

"We started hanging out every day, drinking and smoking weed. One night he had some smack and asked me if I wanted to try it. He had a way of making things OK, you know. Before I realized it, I was stealing to support both of us. But that's not the worst." Brandi's voice cracked and quivered.

Hunter saw her life shattering in his head. He knew, but he had to ask. She had to tell her story. "What did he make you do, Brandi?"

"Never mind, darling, why don't we go to your place. I can show you a good time."

"How about we have another drink." Hunter motioned to the bartender. After a few more Brandi got talking again.

"Eventually, he was pimping me out — to his friends at first, then the streets. I tried to run away, many times, but he would threaten me, and when I told him I didn't care, then my family. He was crazy, possessed. But not so long ago, after he passed out after one of his beatings, I just took his drugs and cash and I never looked back."

The cigarette smoke travelled from her mouth and out her nostrils. Hunter bit his lower lip, which he always did when he was thinking.

"Brandi, you know he won't let you go. You ripped him off, for one. He thinks he has an image to keep up. You should leave town."

"I just want to get fucked up!" Brandi motioned to the bartender. "Two more shots!"

As the night wore on Hunter lost interest in Brandi. He couldn't get Cate out of his head. But Brandi was very drunk. He needed to get her home all right.

"Do you want me to call a cab?"

"Well, I was hoping we could get out of here and party at your place. The night is young!"

"I'll drive you in my truck. Are you coming?" Hunter pointed to the front door.

"I need to use the restroom first."

Those stripper stilettos are sexy, Hunter mumbled as Brandi wobbled away. Oh, stop it! You don't need to get involved — she is drunk. Just take her home. Hunter breathed in Cate's smell, still in his shirt. He couldn't tell if it was the shots or Cate that made his head spin.

"Hey buddy it's closing time! Can you get your girl and head out?" The bartender scowled at him.

Hunter went back into the back and knocked on the bathroom door. "Brandi, we need to go. I will give you a lift. Brandi, come on!"

Hunter creaked the door open to the lady's room. Been a while since I have been in here! "Brandi, can we wrap this up? Brandi? Shit! Help! I need some help in here!" Brandi was sprawled on the floor of the stall. Hunter screamed down the hall. "Call an ambulance — she is overdosing!"

"Oh, fuck!" The bartender ran for his phone to call 911.

"Brandi, come on wake the fuck up!" Hunter shook the unresponsive girl, who was barely breathing. The loose belt slipped from her arm, the heroin soaring through her veins. The needle was still in her hand. Hunter propped against the wall and closed his eyes.

"Lisa! Hurry come here!" Wendy hollered down the hallway.

"What's going on Wendy? Woah! What happened? Is he dead?"

"No, silly – he's just high. He was getting a little rough, so I suggested we shoot up. You know to take the edge off." Wendy presented a needle filled with brown liquid. "I told him to go first. I just wanted to smoke a joint. Here help me move him on his side." Wendy knelt and started searching with cold efficiency.

"I'm not touching him! Stan will kill us!" Lisa put both hands up.

"Listen, I'm tired of them scum bags touching me, asking me to do what their wives won't do. We're being chewed up and spit out. Stan is getting the money. I'm taking what's mine. Here, hold on to the smack. We can sell it."

Lisa held the baggy far out in front of her.

"Put it in your pocket. Now, help me roll him over before he wakes up. There it is." Wendy held up his wallet. "Asshole. He wanted to give me twenty bucks — look at all these bills. Here's your cut."

"Sir, move please. Get the Narcan quick." The medics moved Brandi to the stretcher and worked on her. "Is she with you? What's her name?" The paramedic slipped the IV in with exact precision.

Hunter halted and jumped back to the present. "Her name's Brandi — we just met. I was going to give her a ride home, that's all I know. Will she be OK?"

"She's coming around slowly. It's a good thing you found her when you did. John, she is ready to transport."

"Brandi, Its Hunter. Hang in there." Hunter's warm hand grazed her cold arm.

"Stan…. Are you coming with me?" Brandi's raspy voice asked.

Hunter stopped, then followed the paramedics outside, and watched them lift her with ease into the ambulance. The lights and horns blaring put Hunter into a trance like state. His knees locked as the ambulance vanished into the night. Stan. I need to find out what she knows. And he dissolved into memory.

Lisa was standing over her mom, shaking her. The empty pill bottle rolled onto the floor from her mother's lifeless fingers, Lisa's spirit levitated with tremendous force. Leaving her body once again, guiltlessly soaring away like her mom's spirit. Why should she care? Mom was going to leave her alone with Stan. She had abandoned Lisa with her abuser.

Her mother's pupils plunged back into her head. She went limp, her gray pallor and white eyes making her look like an alien. Lisa ran for the phone, but she couldn't remember any numbers.

Then she saw the strawberry red lights bouncing off the windows. Who had called 911? Were they coming to her house to get her mother?

"Don't die on me, Mom, please. I forgive you!"

This couldn't be happening again. Hunter latched on the wheel and drove, fast.

Cate's hands were shaking when she hung up from Donna's call. They were shorthanded at the hospital, and Donna was "willing to look past her indiscretions" for some immediate help.

"This is my chance!" Cate set her coffee cup down.

Smokey darted in front of Cate, almost tripping her on the way to her closet.

"His clothes are gone, Smokey!"

Smokey scolded Cate with his high-pitched meow, sitting on her uniform so she couldn't get ready. Cate was still distracted from the evening before, the lovemaking and the fight. She could still smell him on her sheets.

In the shower, Cate tried to wash her stress away. The soap draining down her body lathered like an embrace. She wished she could have met Hunter another time or place. He scared her. Why didn't you hold him tighter, Cate? But it wasn't right. And now she had to keep it together.

Part of Cate wanted to tell Donna where to take a flying leap. Donna was bending the rules only because she needed help. After her shower she swallowed her hormone pill and the last pill in her underwear drawer. Screw Donna, I need this to get through the day. She'll be watching.

Lisa hated herself. She had become numb from the years of abuse from Stan; It took decades for the deadness to fade. The resentment still came quickly, with anger. She held her mother's suicide note, asking Stan to "take care of your sister." There was no turning back. If her mother died, it would cement her future as a lifetime of pain. Lisa wadded up the note and threw it in the wastebasket. Her mother wouldn't leave her so easily.

"Young lady, what did your mom take?" The paramedic's eyes searched hers for an answer. His pity radiated around her. Oh, how Lisa resented his precise awareness of her femaleness.

His big rough hands compressed on her mother's chest. They shoved an alien tube down her throat to give her life again, whether she wanted it or not.

As they took her away, her mothers' ring rubbed against Lisa's arm, as if she was reaching out. Lisa ignored it.

Mom was in the hospital for a while after that. Lisa's perverted stepfather made sure of it. He wanted Lisa's mother committed to the psychiatric ward long term for an evaluation. His motive being to use drugs, drink, and bring home his lovers. But Lisa was glad when the springs on the bed started squeaking. For that night, at lease, she knew his unclean fingers wouldn't be on her. Short-term security.

At the Emergency Room, everyone seemed to be staring at Hunter. The hospital staff scurrying around made his head spin. Where are you, Brandi?

Cate was sweating as she left Donna's office. She had scolded her in a condescending tone while Cate just nodded. Cate knew Donna really needed her there. Otherwise, she wouldn't have compromised. It was funny how people only bend the rules in their favor.

Picking up her schedule of rounds for the shift, Cate headed out. The smell of bleach filled her nostrils, and her shoes made a squeaking noise as she stepped down the newly buffed hallway. Donna had made sure she didn't have access to pain medicine and for once she didn't care.

Hunter peered into each hospital room window to find Brandi. He should have asked someone. But he didn't know if the police were involved. The police were not very sympathetic to his kind. He stayed back in the hall when he finally found the room, where nurses were settling her in.

"What happened to this poor girl?" An orderly asked as she changed the IV bag.

"Look at her arms; they tell the whole story. The paramedics were able to save her."

"I hope she gets the help she needs. Come on, we're behind."

Hunter stepped away from the door and quietly tiptoed in as they left. Brandi was a shell of the vibrant young woman she had been hours ago. Her skin was gray and the tracks on her arm were revealed by the short sleeves of the hospital gown. It probably wasn't the first time she had been here.

Then a familiar voice interrupted his reflections.

"Hunter? What are you doing here?" Cate's blood ran cold. She sat down her medical supplies. "Do you know this young woman?"

Hunter tried to speak but the words were jammed in his throat. It seemed like an eternity since he met this elegant creature. Her presence demanded respect. And he was defenseless.

"I've been better." Hunter purposefully put distance in his voice. He was irritated that she acted unaffected by their lovemaking.

Femmes have it so much easier! Hunter scowled. They had a hidden power over their lovers, and he wished he was immune. A woman's power could be a gift bestowed on the right man, but Cate was manipulating him, and holding back at the same time. When a femme completely trusts her partner it's an exchange of power, but she wants the same in return. Her trust must be held delicately and treasured. Cate had pierced his armor, but she didn't care.

"Hunter." She placed her long, well-manicured nails on his arm. "What's going on? You're safe with me."

"REALLY?" Hunter scoffed. "You were sure in no hurry to have me leave!"

Cate shook her head. "Not in front of a patient." They darted out into the hallway.

"Safe with you - that's a fucking joke!" Hunter shoved her calming hand away.

"If you haven't noticed I'm at work. Keep your voice down!" Cate whispered through scrunched teeth.

Hunter tried to change the subject. He wanted her on the defensive. Call it revenge.

"How did you get your job back?" Hunter tried to act interested, neutral.

"I'm working on it." Cate was a pro at evasion. "So — why are you here? Did something happen?"

"Long story. A girl I was hanging out with had an accident, so I came up here to check on her." He flopped back in the uncomfortable plastic chair, crossing his arms across his chest.

"Well, you didn't waste any time finding someone else. And what a catch!" Cate was surprised at her outburst.

"You made it perfectly clear that it was time for me to go. I wanted to stay."

"Looks like I dodged a bullet. It seems you have no problem testing out your dick twice in one night!" Cate's voice echoed off the hospital walls. They were drawing attention to themselves. "I have to go."

"Cate! Wait!"

CHAPTER 6

Hunter was exhausted. He wasn't going to find out anything more from Brandi tonight, or ever, and she was stable for now. Hunger took over. He forced himself to the parking garage and started his truck.

Brandi's words revealed one thing. Stan was still around, and nothing had changed. Hunter tried to put it aside. He had to focus on his work. He was behind on his writing and his editor would be on his case. It was time to work on himself. And he was too wired to sleep.

Sitting at home at his computer, Hunter couldn't concentrate, so he put on some music to inspire his words. No words were coming. Think, Hunter, think! Love always came at a cost. For Hunter to give a part of himself, he needed something back. He understood and became sympathetic with the vampires, werewolves; they were the real underdogs. Like them, he wanted more. Marking his territory, he deserved praise and admiration. Rejection is brutal but it helps with writing. Use Cate. Use this feeling.

But this time he couldn't write it out. Cate was always within reach in the lustful corners of his mind. Her body was a canvas that he wanted to explore and cherish. He craved to get lost in her gaze, to adore the way the corners of her mouth would turn upward when she was thinking. All these mysteries he needed to untangle with her. He wished he was still at the hospital. Everyone deserves a second chance.

Hunter sipped his hot coffee slowly. Everyone abandoned him. But he was still here. Then the words came, exploding off his fingers onto the pages. The distraction was calming, comforting, passing his emotions on to his characters. He lived covertly in each one. They represented a time in his life when people and encounters failed him. They breathed because he survived.

His groin distracted him with its itching and burning. It was all part of the healing process, he reminded himself. Doctor Thatcher had given Hunter hope, but everything took time. His face was starting to become narrow and defined, hair spouting and growing in patches. His legs were gaining muscles and both arms had masculine lines and veins veering off. Hunter had transitioned to survive, and he was finding his own truth.

"Hey Lisa, Old Man Bob is taking us swimming at the lake. Want to come?"

Lisa didn't trust the neighbor boys. But summer was ending, and she was restless. Her mother would be furious if she found out. "Lisa, it's not natural for a grown man to hang around kids all the time."

She would just stay away from him and enjoy the lake on this beautiful summer afternoon.

"Come up front here and sit by me, Lisa." Bob patted the seat next to him and blew cigarette smoke through his teeth. All the other seats were taken, and part of her knew it was a strategic move on his part. A familiar sinking sensation formed in her stomach. Lisa slid into the empty front seat and jammed herself so close to the car door she would fall out if it opened suddenly.

"You look mighty grown up in your swimming suit." Bob licked his lips with a glance at her budding chest and crushed out his cancer stick.

Lisa realized this was a bad idea. When the van came to a stop she dashed out and ran toward the water. She was running from home, the neighbor kids, Bob… but most of all, from her body and herself. The water was cool and clean against her skin. Almost even purifying. But she would never be clean again.

"Hey kids, I have some sandwiches if you're hungry!" Bob's bellow echoed across the vast water. "Lisa. I can put some suntan lotion on you, so those sexy shoulders won't get burned."

What a fucking pervert, Lisa dragged her tongue across her teeth. I'm only fifteen years old. He is sick! Lisa snatched a sandwich and went to the other side of the lake. While she was skipping rocks, a cold shadow passed over her.

"I brought you a beer." Bob's long fat fingers were wrapped around the bottle, highlighting his grungy fingernails.

Lisa didn't want to take it. But she had learned to depend on it.

"Sure, why not?"

"That's my girl." Bob said with confidence as he fumbled for another cigarette. "I have some new video games at my house. You know, the kind you kids like nowadays. My wife works the night shift...why don't you come over and I'll show you my new moves?" Bob leered and blew smoke rings in perfect circles.

Lisa stared him up and down with total disgust. The fucked-up part was that this type of behavior didn't even faze her. All it did was reaffirm her contempt for humans, especially men. The way he would smack his lips together and clutch his crotch made her ill. She had visions of taking her hidden pocketknife and shoving it in his throat.

Lisa waited until he started to slur his words and eventually passed out. Then she knew it was safe to go to the bathroom in the bushes. She sure as fuck wasn't comfortable pulling her swimsuit down around him.

As she squatted to pee, her focus came to the birds swooping down and plucking defenseless prey from the ground. She decided that it was time to go home. Jerking her swimsuit back up, she attempted to move quietly around Bob to start the long walk back to the main road where she would hitchhike home. Lisa had almost made it when a meaty fist shot out and netted her bare ankle.

"Where are you going, doll?" Bob's breath reeked of alcohol. Hefting to his feet, he pushed Lisa against a rock and slammed his tongue down her throat. Heat squished against her as he pinched Lisa's breasts with a hungry, painful squeeze. The blood flushed his face and his pants. He was so close to her she could smell stale cigarette smoke and the musky odor of other women.

Climbing deep down inside her inner strength, Lisa doubled up her fists. "Get your fucking hands off me!" Lisa's hands exploded from her wrists and landed several blows to Bob's face. For a moment, his face morphed in and out, merging with Stan's. His silver tooth reflected the intense summer sunlight, blinding her for an instant.

Hunter wove his story into the page, smirking with satisfaction that karma paid Bob a visit later. He had heard from the grapevine that Bob was caught with an underage girl some years ago. The girl's mother shot him in the courtroom in front of everyone. Maybe I should write her and see if I can interview her for some book material. In Hunter's eyes, she should have walked free.

Nervous sweat made Cate's uniform stick in unwanted places. She grew tired of quiet whispers and pointed looks, but as long as she stayed clean, Donna let her keep working. Still, Cate was eager to help with patients. It was just the distraction she needed. Donna let it be known no pills could be in Cate's possession. Her colleagues were an extra set of eyes for the control freak supervisor. Yet Cate still connected to patients suffering physical or emotional pain. Her own self-discovery and healing were mirrored in their mutual stories and a zest for survival.

A couple of months had passed, and work was going well. One thing seemed to be absent for Cate, however. She missed the physical and emotional connection she had experienced with Hunter. She needed some strong arms to hold her and tell her that everything would be OK. Looking back, Cate was disappointed with herself. The sexual encounter between them was electric and full of chemistry, But Cate had made it impossible for him to stay. Reaching down and touching his penis brought back all the unease and frustration of her own impotence as Edward. Between that and dredging up the man who attacked her, she had just run away. Hunter isn't like him. Why couldn't I see that?

Hunter was beginning to go stir crazy. He did somehow find the energy to shower and fix some lunch between writing and suffering over writing. Depression was hovering, waiting to launch an attack. His hormone treatments were beginning to peak, and his aggression was just under the surface, ready to explode at any given moment. Pent up sexual frustration was making it difficult to concentrate. The weird thing about it was his new prothesis wanted to expand, but it couldn't.

"I'm a fucking Ken doll!" he swore, emasculated as Lisa and even now as Hunter.

Fresh air was the remedy. Driving around the city with no place to go, Hunter had the urge to swing by Cate's house. But a small part of him knew Cate wasn't ready for him, and he was afraid it wasn't his job to convince her. She had to figure it out on her own.

Smokey was faithfully surveying for Cate at the window, jarring his head to open the curtain and check out the wildlife outside while he waited. Once she got inside, the house seemed empty, even with the loyal cat.

Cate loved Smokey, but she didn't understand why he still had affection for Gwen, why he snuggled right up to her, even though she was so cruel to Cate. Gwen betrayed everyone with her lies. She would never forget the afternoon Edward came home early from work to surprise Gwen and take her out to dinner. When he walked into their bedroom and saw her with another man.

"Don't look at me that way, Edward, this is all your fault. I thought that I married a man, not a woman!"

Smokey bumped against her, begging for treats. Cate reluctantly started dinner.

Hunter pulled over for a coffee to collect his thoughts. Dilapidated buildings surrounded him, the years of neglect and poverty hanging stagnant in the air.

Walking into a seedy diner, Hunter scanned the area, always on alert. He preferred to sit away from others. Every corner he would look, faces would melt into Stan's profile, scents would trigger a panic attack. Lisa didn't understand that Hunter could protect them now, and her tears and terrors plagued him. He had to meld Lisa with Hunter, to absorb her, but he was too weary to consider how. He needed coffee.

Slurping the magic brew, heat and caffeine slowly brought him back to life. The daily paper was folded neatly on the table, the headline jumping out at him, black and bold.

Local Girl Found in River.

The hairs on Hunter's neck stood up against his skin.

"Would you like something to eat this afternoon? A sandwich, perhaps?" The waitress spoke through thin lips, tapping her pencil on the table.

"Uh, no thanks."

"I met that girl. She ran the streets around here. Candi? Brenda? But you know how people talk."

Hunter stiffened like a statue, afraid to move. Images of the drunken night at the bar played in his head.

He placed a couple of dollars on the table and walked out. The air was heavy and foggy. How he hated Stan.

Lisa had just come home from a softball game and was looking through the shelves in her room for a CD she had borrowed from a friend. A small plastic bag fell out from behind a book she had just moved, landing on her bed. Inside was some fine white powder. Fear began to rise inside her, and she tamped down the urge to flush the drugs down the toilet.

A familiar smell surrounded her, the kind that sticks in your nose and waters your eyes.

"You found my shit. Do you want to do some?" Stan's voice was cool as a cucumber.

Asshole! How could he let me take the fall for this? "Get out of my room. you freak!"

Stan's eyes turned to stone. Stalking toward her, she could sense his anger flooding her space. He was oozing with contempt. Lisa sent him over the edge.

His body odor was ripe and pungent as he blocked her up against the wall.

"Listen here, you little bitch! The only freak I see around here is you! Don't worry, I'll get you back on track, feeling like a woman should."

Lisa shuddered and almost vomited as he smacked his crusty lips. She was thankful the boards were creaking. Upstairs someone was home.

"I'll deal with you later!" He seized the bag and disappeared to his room.

According to the paper, Brandi had ripped off the wrong person. Whoever it was had hunted her down, raped and murdered her. Hunter would bet money that Stan had been involved. Last he heard Stan was serving time for robbery. Was he out of prison? One thing Hunter did know—he wasn't running from Stan this time. He would find him and face him. For Brandi. For Lisa. And for himself.

Cate carried her brown bag lunch into the staff lounge. Normally she hated impersonal chatter over her sandwich, but today she needed human interaction. She tried to look disinterested as her coworker Jane approached.

"Hello, Cate. How are things going since you've been back?" Jane huffed.

Cate didn't trust her. She knew divulging any information to her would open the floodgates of gossip. "Nothing exciting. Donna is watching me like a hawk."

"Can you really blame her? I mean, how many chances can one person get? Anyway, I wanted to ask you something. Do you mind?" Jane raised her eyebrows, as if she was looking for Cate to object.

"Well Jane, I have a feeling you'll ask whether I do or not." Cate spoke with sarcasm.

Jane proceeded with her interrogation. "Well, I don't mean to pry but a while back we had a trans patient. Do you remember him? Or is it her?" Jane was delighted in her secret. "Rumor has it, well, you guys were close. I defended you, of course. I wanted to protect you."

Cate chewed her food vigorously. She would answer with caution.

"I meet many patients. I don't recall a trans person." Cate hated it when she had to lie.

"Cate, it was at the same time as your last relapse. Everyone knows."

"Everyone knows what, Jane?"

Jane sat her fork down. "Don't make me say it, Cate."

"I'm interested in what you think you know." Cate was shooting daggers at the other woman. She was like a dog on a bone.

"We're all aware of your alternative lifestyle. It must have been difficult to remain hidden all those years. So, naturally you were drawn to your patient. Hunter was his name, right?"

Cate threw her napkin down in horror. "Alternative lifestyle? You can assume all day long. I don't owe you any kind of explanation. You're just one of Donna's suits." Cate was proud of her newfound strength.

"Cate, I'm shocked and saddened that you would think I've any kind of motive. Yes, Donna did ask me to keep an eye out for you. She wanted to make you wouldn't be tempted again."

By now Cate was seething with fury. If Donna recruited a spy, it should be someone of better moral caliber. Jane wasn't as perfect as she acted. She was always flirting and prancing around the doctors while her diligent and unassuming husband waited for her at home.

"I need to do my rounds, Jane. If you have an issue with my personal choices, I suggest looking at your own. Good day." Cate tossed her half-eaten lunch in the bin. Her patients needed her.

† † †

Hunter tugged on his cigarette, a little angry with himself that he had started smoking again. The heat cogged his lungs and spread comfort through him. Blowing the smoke out like a dragon helped to release some of the tension.

He was mentally preparing himself to look for Stan. All the seedy hotels, bars, and drug houses needed to be checked.

Stan had to be stopped and Hunter was up for the task. It was for Brandi, but most of all, Lisa. After months of taking hormones, his biceps were more defined, chest muscles were bulging, his calves had become rock solid. Hunter was ready to unleash his fury. Hunter came across an old hunting knife and strapped it to his belt.

Hunter ran his fingers down the scars on his chest. His fur and muscle made him grateful. Losing Lisa's breasts meant finding his true essence. In Lisa's body he would have drowned in the bottom of the river like Brandi, never to reach the surface. Hunter had lost so much time to rage. It had consumed him throughout adulthood, a lonely black abyss perched over him, ready to demolish him at any moment. Avenging Lisa – avenging Brandi became the new quest.

Hunter smoothed his ballcap down tight and adjusted his sleeves. He would go undercover and slowly creep up on Stan. He had some ideas as to where he would start. He knew Stan's usual haunts. Can't teach an old dog new tricks.

As a teenager, Stan would drag Lisa around from drug house to drug house. Sometimes she would get lucky and convince him she was sleeping, staying in the car to avoid his perverted friends. Anger and lust would spin in their eyes, creating a lethal combination.

Once she was older, he would take her in whether she was asleep or not, belittling Lisa as bait to pass around to his drug buddies, selling her for money or a dime bag of heroin. She had survived by disassociating and being quick with her fists. She had also met the woman she desperately wanted to avoid becoming. Wendy, who thought she loved Stan. Wendy, who loved the drugs. Wendy, who never fought, and didn't care to.

It had been a long time since Hunter had seen Wendy. She had witnessed enough of Wendy's troubles to suspect nothing good was going on. But Lisa couldn't save her. The only thing she could do was sometimes take Wendy's turn when payment time came around. After a string of abusive boyfriends, her children ended up in foster care for their own protection. He had heard she had survived two suicide attempts, too. Lisa's heart had reached out to her. The truth behind her desperation was textbook. Stan's addicts devoured her soul. She and the drugs he controlled were her only escape. Hunter was going to start with Wendy. If she was still alive, she could help him find Stan.

As he drove the buildings started to change shape; unkept, abandoned, dirt yards, cars on blocks stripped of metal and copper for drug money. Any kids on these streets faced drug dealers, prostitutes, pimps, death, and chaos. Their future was almost always set-in stone before they were born. In a weird way Hunter fit right in. Lisa was brought up in this dysfunction and she knew how to cope. Over time, without the mayhem, Lisa couldn't function. Hunter sometimes thought that humans crave peace, but once they see a glimmer of it, they become bored without the struggle. Struggle. That was where Hunter found himself now, out of the disfunction, but deep in the battle of creating himself.

After a few hours of driving around Hunter pulled over for a smoke. All the city people hurried around to get back to their unfulfilling lives. Cate was on his mind, as always. A tingling sensation shot through his body when he thought of her, like skipping rocks on a clear lake. Hunter missed her. Cate's touch was gentle and wild. She wasn't easy. But in comparison, everything else was drab.

Flicking his cigarette out the window, Hunter considered going home for the night. The sun had turned to a flash of red. It was in the dying rays of the day that he saw her.

Wendy had a sunken face that made her look like a patient with a terminal illness. Ratty hair suggested days since she had showered. Her clothes hung on her body, unflattering and torn.

Hunter observed with pity as she twirled her soft hair around her ring finger, this shadow of a woman was mindlessly tangling her dirty hair in twists, like she always had when she was nervous.

Hunter's heart ached for her. Years on the streets had taken its toll.

"Wendy! Hey Wendy!" He beckoned her with his hand, and her head swung slowly toward him, the gaze vacant. She was high. Hunter was going to have to talk her language.

"How much for a good time?" Hunter could barely get the words out.

"How much do you have?" Wendy laughed, but her void eyes didn't reflect any humor.

"We can talk about that later. Get in the truck."

"Look, buddy! I don't know where you think you're at, but I can have your neck slit in an instant."

Her teeth were visible and her once light eyes black as night.

"Calm down, Wendy, I just want to talk. Shit!" He fucked up and said her name again.

"How... how do you know my name?" Wendy demanded.

Hunter was rapping his fingers nervously against the steering wheel. "Stan."

The anger in her eyes changed to fear. "What the fuck do you know about Stan?"

"Look, all I need to say is Burrows Avenue." Hunter hoped this would jog her memory. This was the street they were taken to years ago. On this street their souls were sold to the guy holding the bag of powder.

Wendy was flustered. "Lisa? Do…you know her? She told you about me?"

Hunter was mortified; he knew that he didn't look like Lisa. But his voice must sound familiar to her. "Wendy, it's me. I'm Lisa…well, I was. I want to find Stan. Do you know where he is?"

"Lisa, what have you done to yourself? Is this because of your brother?" Wendy came to the door of the truck to examine him more closely.

Wendy placed her hand upon his face stroking his beard, looking at him in amazement and wonder. She opened the door of the truck to rest against him, obviously not wanting to be overheard by the others on the corner who were now eyeballing them.

"You know I can't tell you where he is. Stan will kill me."

"What if I told you he has killed someone. By the way, my name is Hunter now." For some weird reason he didn't mind Wendy calling him Lisa.

"Lisa…. Hunter. You finally went through with it. You were so unhappy. We would stay up and talk for hours. Remember? Over the years I've wondered about you. You look good as a man."

Wendy fondled Hunter's inner thigh and squeezed him hard. Suddenly, Hunter wanted to get as far away as he could. Wendy was doing what she had been taught. She needed money to numb her pain, and she only knew one way to get it… friend or not.

"Wendy." He gently removed her hand. "I only wanted to know where Stan is."

"Listen, last I knew he was staying at that friend's house. The pusher we knew. He's violent. If the word gets out that I gave up his location…. So, all I can say is west side. You can figure it out."

"Thank you."

"Now, was you serious about some money exchange? I can cut you a deal."

Hunter didn't want to let Wendy know that even talking to her, much less smelling her unwashed body, made him physically ill. She had enough disappointments to deal with already.

"I need to go, Wendy. Take care of yourself."

"You're just like every other man in my life. Useless! You were a freak as Lisa and you're a freak now!" Wendy's nostrils flared; her anger as red as her badly dyed stringy hair.

She charged down the street with the same infantile stomp she had as a teenager. The truth was, he felt sorry for her. Her dreams of becoming a dancer were gone from the first time Stan put her out, his newest innocent. Why did men like the virgin types? Are they in love with the notion that they're the first? Dipping their seed into a fantasy world of their control and desires, only to discard you like a carcass waiting for the crows to take you out of your misery.

The sad thing about it was Hunter wanted to save her, but knew it was far too late. Hunter was barely able to take care of himself. Besides, look what had happened to Brandi. He did the only thing he could do. He drove back to the west side.

CHAPTER 7

Cate was up early the next morning with her typical routine. The hormone pills went down her throat sideways and almost came back up but finally settled, repressing any remnant of Edward. Still, they were beginning to feel like a ball and chain. She wasn't safe anymore. Work was a prison, with all the staff and Donna wanting her to fail. She feared the blackness that was in front of her, knowing where it would ultimately lead.

Cate wanted to be reckless, to act on something besides fear, to break out of her isolation. Pills had always numbed the pain, but she didn't want to be numb anymore—she wanted to experience things. A month ago, she would have swallowed a handful and washed them down with a bottle of scotch, but that wasn't enough anymore. She certainly needed more intimacy than her cat could provide. She wanted someone to be there when things got hard. I need to get out of this house. Maybe I will see Hunter.

Hunter had stayed at a seedy motel in the heart of Stan's stomping grounds that night. Slowly sipping his morning coffee, he watched a storm blow in, trees shaking and wailing in rhythm, like a sad melody. As he was pulling on his underwear, Hunter grimaced at his penis. Nothing was working the way he had hoped. He was still trapped, his body unable to release the way he had imagined. He snorted – a pitiful Ken doll who would never really love Barbie. Ridiculous, but it was true. And memories of being Lisa kept emerging without warning.

"Lisa, why do you have boys' underclothes on? I see the waistband."

The million-dollar question asked by everyone in Lisa's teenage years.

He tucked his shirt into his jeans. Hunter had slowly lost his hope for humanity. Or maybe, truth be told, he had lost hope for himself. Like a caterpillar stuck between the cocoon and his butterfly wings.

Hunter missed the warmth he had with Susie; the need for it almost crippled him. At the same time, he doubted he really knew how to be intimate. He was still terrified of the darkness within him. In this conquest to find our second spirit and become one soul, must we lose ourselves? He had to find Stan to purge that darkness.

Hunter found his keys and headed out. Stan loved two things: young girls and drugs. This is where Hunter began, cruising the streets. The reality of it made him sick, but this is what he had to do, and he was prepared to do it. As he drove closer to downtown the colors and graffiti became more prominent, streets scattered with runaways. This would-be Stan's hunting grounds.

To find a predator, you must become one. These streets were a whole different world. Merciless and volatile, they turned everyone into a survivor. Hunter channeled Lisa's ability to disconnect and shut off his emotions so he could navigate the unwanted and untouchables, a lost society in the grip of desperation.

After hours of talking to pimps, hookers, and junkies, Hunter's chest was heavy with despair and darkness. He couldn't escape it. This void, the pain, and desolation had excreted into his bones, took him back to terrors he had tried so hard to leave behind. His anxiety levels were high. The dilapidated liquor store around the corner beckoned him to crawl back inside the bottle. He went in, not thinking about it.

The first shot was always the best, heating his blood, pumping through him in a wash of relief. It drove the bullshit farther away. Years of failed partnerships, friendships, and alliances with numerous people had crumbled in the wake of alcoholism. It wasn't completely their fault. His insecurity and fear created a wall too high to scale. Only the bottle understood him, loved him. His anger at the world for their inability to ease his pain ultimately ended in isolation, his greatest fear.

The brown paper was teasing him with its contents. He had to keep a straight head, but the whiskey paved a path to forgetting. Maybe someday I'll have the courage to face my demons—or at least have dinner with them. Hunter laughed to himself as he cracked the seal and took a sip.

An hour later, the colors around him were mixing like a kaleidoscope. He knew that he was intoxicated. Trails of lights from cars were blinding him. He located a parking lot to regroup for a few hours. Stan was within his reach; he could almost smell him like basement musk on your clothes, a scent that Hunter despised. It reminded him of poverty and misery. As he closed his eyes, it started to thunder. The storm was here.

Cate paced back and forth. Work had been a disaster today, but it was finally the weekend. Donna was circling her, and sidekick Jane was there to twist the knife. She poured a drink and rubbed her finger around the ice cubes.

She was tempted to go into town for a free concert from a local band. Maybe she would run into Hunter. It was a long shot, but a girl could dream. Her mind was aching thinking about their encounter. The memory of his fragrance rose, his body spread across her, his hands caressing her and keeping her safe. Why wasn't that enough for her? Cate was frustrated with herself.

Cate threw caution to wind and started to dress. Her stockings felt silky and sultry against her skin. She loved how her lipstick soaked into her full red lips, making her confident sexy and alive. Her diamond necklace settled seductively against her defined breastbone. She applied perfume to her pulse points. Cate didn't know exactly what she would find but her soul needed a release. The inner conflict and work stress were tearing her in to a million little pieces.

Cate secured her keys and purse, giving Smokey a pat on top of his head. "Don't worry, Smokey, I'll be back before you know it."

She turned the radio up full blast and let her car take her wherever she would land.

Hunter awoke in the parking lot to a fight, a pimp slapping his girl for stealing. The chivalrous part of him wanted to help, but the reality was, if he helped her, she would turn on him in a minute. They always went back. It was a sad lesson he had learned growing up. He drove off in search of coffee.

He had sobered up enough to know that he had to focus. Stan was nearby.

The DJ on his car radio announced a free concert in town. Any big drug dealer would be there. It was a huge opportunity to make tons of money with a great cover from the crowd. Hunter headed home to shower and rest. He would find him there. Tonight, he had to be sharp.

On the way home to prepare, it started to rain again, and the droplets splashed and spread across his windshield like mercury on a plate. At home he found a beer next to a week-old sandwich in the fridge. He put on some soft music to relax a bit. As he undressed to get in the shower the trees were banging against the window. A change was in the air. Tonight, was the night for revenge.

Cate parked and zigzagged up to the entrance, trying to keep her balance in her highest heels. Men's eyes fell upon her. Her dress was tight and revealing. The joke was on them; this sexy siren had no interest in anyone except Hunter. But she would let them look as much as they wanted.

The crowd was beginning to gather, the concert should be starting soon. The young couples made her jealous, she wanted Hunter there with her, his big strong hands pressed against her waist, his pelvis straight and hard against her. The energy from the evening would pulse before them. In the darkness of the music, you can be whatever you want.

"Can I buy you a drink?" A rough voice echoed in Cate's ears.

Cate rotated to say no when she spotted this rugged man with an uncanny resemblance to Hunter. Same large hands, same space between his front teeth. His identical blue-green eyes almost burned her.

"Yes, thank you." Cate was intrigued and amused. Maybe Hunter was closer than she thought.

Hunter stripped slowly, preparing to shower, looking at his body in awe and wonderment. Was all that really his? The needle made the familiar popping noise as he poked it into his leg. His new penis might not work yet, but he was a man, no doubt. He slicked back his hair and combed his goatee.

On the outside, no traces of Lisa were apparent. But on the inside, she was running rampant. He found it odd that he couldn't escape Lisa, even in moments like this; she was in every corner of his mind. Hunter reserved all his strength and protection around her like a bubble, waiting for the true and genuine transformation that needed to occur. He fought the tears escaping down his face.

At least his body was beginning to heal. After the shower, he tweaked his package toward the left of his underwear. Ironically, he imagined himself surrounded by a fortress, his penis clenched in a locked fist.

Hunter splashed the brown liquid in a glass and pounded it back. It sent chills down his spine. Alcohol helped. His confidence would soar, and his arrogance was right around the corner. Another shot filled his head. Hunter elected to leave while he had his wits about him.

Old familiar songs played on the radio. Cate was coming in waves in and out of his memory. Within reach but so far away. But first, Stan. If Stan was to be found this evening was prime time. The rain had stopped, and the summer heat was like dirt balls exploding under his feet, sweat rolling down his face and arms as he passed the sign for the free concert at a local carnival. He parked close to the entrance.

As he stepped onto the fairground, he passed a young couple necking and groping each other. Their effortless intimacy was irritating. Hunter was blinded by all the lights. He sat down on a bench and lit a smoke. He wanted a beer but decided he needed to stay sharp. After some time, he was startled by a raspy baritone voice. He spun – it was Cate, but its depth contradicted her angelic face, deceiving in its pitch.

"Why, thank you, handsome, I would love to ride the Ferris wheel."

The air began to shift, and the atmosphere sucked Hunter's poise out into the wind.

Then he saw him – "handsome." He could smell him from here – Lisa's memory filling in the details. Stan's sink was pooling into his pores and etched inside Hunter's mouth, the putrid stench of his soul that only Hunter could detect.

Cate touched Stan's arm and threw her hair back, and Stan grinned, igniting dangerous flames inside Hunter. He was going to knock that smug smile and sliver tooth off Stan's face.

Stan would soon know his strength and power. In due time. Right now, he followed the trail of Cate's laughter. Stan strutted down the aisle with walls of people that parted like the Red Sea. He had a dangerous walk — no one wanted to get in his way.

Cate had been drinking, and Stan must have kept them coming. The ruse was in place. Stan's watchful leer telegraphed his intentions. He was grooming her as he had Lisa and so many others, preparing for the kill. Cate had no idea of the danger she was in. She was oblivious, like an insect drawn to a light and suddenly trapped in a spider's web. This was Stan's aphrodisiac, a ritualistic dance of depravity.

The concert was starting, lights were dimming. Couples were pairing off and getting seats close to one another. Stan marched right past Hunter towards the concert tent, and their eyes locked. His brother had never seen him as Hunter.

Stan's expression was black and lifeless, like a reptile's sinking its teeth into its kill. Hunter's heartbeat pounding inside his ears. He felt a panic attack coming on and took a deep breath. Stay in your body, Hunter. It's OK, Lisa. He doesn't see us as anything but competition! Still, he floated above the lights and the music of the band for a minute, nearly gone.

A loud booming laugh filled with overconfidence and conviction shot Hunter back in his body almost instantly. Stan had found a seat and gotten Cate yet another drink, and Hunter could tell from her glazed eyes and slow speech that he had put something in it. When Lisa had friends over, Stan would offer her friends doctored alcohol. She remembered her helplessness and fear.

Night-time was when Lisa was on high alert. Stan's demeanor would darken, his demands increasing. Her brother sucked all the life from the room. Sometimes she was the only one who could see it. One night, she woke up sensing that something wasn't right. All her friends were asleep on the floor in their sleeping bags except Jodi. Smoke and music crept under the door from the hallway, creating the illusion of seduction and passion.

As Lisa carefully creaked Stan's bedroom door it opened an inch. She had to readjust her eyes to take in the terror before her. Stan was taking her friend's clothes off. Jodi was clearly incapacitated, her eyes red and her movements slow and heavy, surrounded by beer bottles, and half-smoked joints. Stan had it all planned out. Lisa was so enraged she stood, immobilized, forced to watch Jodi's rape. She couldn't scream or utter a sound to save her friend. In some sick and twisted way, deep down Lisa was relieved that it wasn't her. This time.

Stan always took what he wanted. Hunter ran his fingers throughout his full goatee. Not this time. He was ready to take his brother down.

"If you really want to party, we can head back to my place. What do you think?" Stan smiled so big the reflection of his sliver tooth bounced off the lights.

"Well, what kind of woman do you think I am? Not tonight, handsome." Cate tried to talk seductively, but her words came out in a slur.

"I won't take no for an answer!" Stan growled.

Stan's vice grip hands clamped down on Cate's wrist. The frenzy in Stan's eyes scared Hunter. He stayed close, but Hunter couldn't blow his cover.

The mood of the evening changed in an instant. Stan pulled Cate towards the parking lot by her arm and hair, her feet leaving drag marks in the gravel. Her face colored with fright and panic. Her fists bounced off his chest, but it was no use – she had been born small for a male, and Stan was much larger.

Hunter followed running toward Stan's pickup. He was too late; Stan had already shoved Cate into the truck. Hunter was close enough to see through the window that Stan had his hand wrapped up in Cate's hair, pinning her head to his lap. She tried to resist him, but it was useless. He sped away, kicking up dirt and gravel in Hunter's face. His legs were beginning to give out on him as he approached his own truck. After a few panicked minutes, Hunter finally was able to catch up to Stan.

They were picking up speed and blowing past stop signs and traffic lights. In the distance Hunter could hear the whistle of a train. If his prediction was correct, Stan had to stop. This could be an opportunity to get Cate out of the car. They approached the train gate just as arms were down, and Stan slammed on the brakes. Soon, the train was screeching by.

This was Hunters only chance. He jumped out of his truck and hurried to the passenger side window, banging on it.

"Cate! Cate! It's me! Get out!"

"Hunter! The door is locked! Help me!"

Stan reached across the cab and restrained Cate by her throat. Then he slowly began to smirk, mocking Hunter as he began to shake Cate like a rag doll.

"Cate, cover your head!" The train had almost passed. Hunter covered up his hand in his shirt and crashed his fist into the passenger window. The pressure from the blow erupted and flung the glass everywhere. Tiny pieces of glass shimmered in the light like diamonds.

The sound of the glass exploding caused Stan to lose his grip on Cate as he covered his own face. She freed herself from his grasp and ran with Hunter to his truck.

As they sped away Stan was coming right on their tail.

"How did you find me?" Cate was talking fast and erratic, struggling to get the words out.

Cate was shuddering and trying to catch her breath. Handfuls of hair fell in her lap from Stan's yanking her around. Black mascara smeared down her high cheekbones. Her hand found Hunter's and squeezed hard, holding on for dear life.

"You have his eyes and hands. I kept hoping it was you. I haven't stopped thinking about you. I wanted to reach out to you. I'm so sorry, Hunter." Cate covered her mouth. "I think I'm going to be sick."

"I'm here now, Cate. Should I pull over?" Hunter asked.

"No, I don't want him to catch up. Hunter, what was he going to do? Kill me? Rape me?"

Hunter saw the fright and anguish in her face. He already knew the answer. How could she have been so stupid? With Stan looking so much like Hunter she was drawn to him like a moth to the flame. But he thought she had better sense than to get so drunk – and let herself be vulnerable to a stranger again.

"Yes, he would rape you. At least. I think he was involved with that girl they found murdered. I'm so glad that I found you." Hunter's voice cracked.

"Can you stay with me tonight? I don't want to be alone." Tears were streaming down her face. Her eyes filled like big blue pools, so inviting.

"Yes, of course," Hunter whispered.

Cate placed her head on Hunter's broad shoulder as they drove. He was aware of the risks going back to Cate's house. She might have told Stan where she lived, somehow. So, he headed down the back roads to his home. The movement of his truck slowly rocked Cate to sleep. She was in and out of consciousness and dream, muttering incoherently and asking what happened, what was wrong with her. Hunter decided to wait to tell the events of the evening until she was more alert. He couldn't help but notice the finger marks on her neck and her torn and tattered clothes.

This beautiful unique creature was violated by Hunter's past. He should have been there earlier. He should have stopped Stan before Cate became his next victim. That bastard will pay for this.

CHAPTER 8

Gliding into the driveway, Hunter carefully placed Cate's head on the head rest as he went to unlock the front door. He switched on the outside light and headed down the stairs. Inside his bedroom he gently laid her down and covered her up. He kissed her softly on her forehead, and Cate opened her eyes.

"Hunter… where are we?" Cate replied confused by her surroundings.

"You're at my home in my bed." Hunter spoke quietly.

"Can you turn the light on? I want to look around."

Hunter reached over her and switched the light on. Cate immediately covered her eyes. "Turn it off! My head is spinning." He did. Hunter wanted her to feel safe.

As Cate took in the room, Hunter went to fix some coffee. He needed a drink, but coffee would keep his head clear. Hunter wasn't used to company. He was very particular about who he let in. It felt strange to have her there, and good.

"Cream and sugar, right?" Hunter said as he put her steamy cup of coffee down on the end table.

Cate half smiled. "You remember. I'm impressed."

"I remember many things." Hunter replied while carefully doctoring up his coffee.

"Well, you failed to mention that you're a writer." Cate motioned to his book on the nightstand with his name stamped on the spine.

Hunter continued with his task. "We've plenty of time to talk about that. You need to rest, and I need to sleep too." Hunter tucked her curl behind her perfect ear eagerly taking the opportunity to stroke her majestic face.

"I didn't thank you properly." Cate sheltered her eyes from Hunter staring directly in front of her holding back the tears. "To be honest all that I recall is going to the concert and having a beer with some man. The next thing I know you yanked me out of his car into your truck. What happened?"

"No need to thank me, I want to protect you. Whoever this person is, he is dangerous and needs to be stopped." Hunter hated lying to Cate, but he wasn't ready to disclose that it was Stan. Maybe she would hate Hunter or worse, assume he was exactly like his brother.

Hunter's heart rate quickened, and his defined jaw line tightened. "I will sleep on the couch. You're safe here. We can talk more about it tomorrow."

"Hunter, I don't think that I can sleep alone. Will you stay until I fall asleep?"

Hunter sat on the edge of the bed and took his motorcycle boots off. He curled up close to Cate. Her hair had a fragrance of crisp clean water, a creek in the wilderness. He slowly ran his fingers down her arm and nuzzled gently until she fell asleep.

The next morning Hunter awoke early to work on some overdue writing. It was hard to concentrate with a beautiful woman sleeping in the next room. His agent has been patient with him so now was the time to produce something of caliber.

This project was a memoir. It wasn't easy, putting your life under a microscope. Being honest about the good and bad was painful and exhausting. And he was a little stuck – he wanted to write about the final confrontation with Stan, so the most important part of his book was on hold. If every person in Hunter's life had become an intricate part of a puzzle, each piece with its own chapter, the most important piece hadn't even happened.

"Good morning, Hunter." Cate said as she closed the bedroom door and tied Hunter's dressing gown around her waist. She was holding her head and grimacing. She still had the aftereffects of the date rape drug in her system.

"Good morning." Hunter chirped, amused, and flattered that Cate was wearing his robe. "Here, take some aspirin." Cate cupped her hand under the faucet to get a drink before he could offer her a glass.

"I must say you look better in my old robe than I do."

"I like your smell. Coffee?" Cate gestured toward the kitchen.

"Of course, let me get it for you." Hunter closed his computer.

"Don't fuss over me. I can get it. Besides, you have a book to write."

Cate sat down with her coffee across from Hunter's computer. She was rubbing her bruised neck and mindlessly touching her scrapes and scratches. "I'm not sure what to say to work." Cate sighed holding her head.

"Can you take any time off?" Hunter proposed.

"I just went back. My credibility isn't the best right now. Anyway, you're busy and I should get home to Smokey." Cate sat her half cup of coffee down.

Hunter stood up quickly. "Listen, call in sick for a couple days until you heal. Your house isn't safe right now. We don't know if he knows where you live. I think you should stay here. We can go get you some clothes and pick-up Smokey. Stay here with me."

"What about your book? Will you be able to work with Smokey and me here?"

"I have written in solitude for so long. Having company would be great!" Hunter's emerald eyes lit up like jewels.

"I would feel safer here." Cate said with gratitude in her voice.

"It's settled then. Get dressed!"

On the drive over Hunter couldn't contain his excitement. Cate was on the phone explaining to work that she had a flu bug and that she wouldn't be coming in. Hunter was torn between worrying about Stan and relishing the fall day and the change in the air. Cate was all right, and she was here.

I'm not letting him steal my moment from me. Hunter thought to himself. Bouncing into Cate's driveway he saw two blue eyes looking at him from the comfort of the windowsill. Smokey was waiting for Cate. Hunter asked for the keys, unlocked the door, and went in first.

"Hunter, I'm scared!" Cate's voice quivered.

"Don't worry, Cate. Hold on to my shirt and stay close to me." Smokey escorted both too. His anxiety level was off the charts, running and meowing into every room. The atmosphere was off in the house, the air stale and heavy. Dirty dishes were stacked in the sink and the trash was ripe. Hunter wanted to get in and out.

"Don't mind my messy house. I had a rough week." Cate was clearly using again, and the house resembled the chaos associated with going on a bender.

"Let's pack your clothes. Get any books or paperwork you need. I will get Smokey. Is his food in the kitchen?" He didn't wait for a reply. Smokey showed him where the food was. Hunter took some cans and found the cat carrier under the table.

"Sorry, Smokey. You will love my house, I promise." Smokey went in on the first try. The cat doesn't want to stay here either. Hunter thought as he latched the kennel door. He headed back up the stairs to see what was taking Cate so long.

"Are you ready to go?" Hunter propped on the door frame catching his breath.

"I love my home Hunter, and now its tainted. Is he watching my every move! Bad enough it was happening at work!" Cate tossed her suitcase on the bed, almost beaten.

Hunter sat down beside her. "I understand. We grew up not feeling safe in our bodies or communities. Your home is your sanctuary. It will be again! You'll be safe in my home for now. We'll figure it out together."

Cate nodded. "Smokey is waiting for us."

"I will be down soon. Give me a minute." Cate went into the bathroom to get her personal items and her hormone kit. She was hesitant about staying with Hunter. The last time she had shared a space was with Gwen and she wasn't sure if she was ready to be under anyone's thumb. Enough of the over thinking. It will be OK.

"Oh, I can't forget Smokey's favorite toy! Probably under my bed."

Cate squatted down to tap under the bed she found a toy mouse and a circular container. Her heart sank as soon as she read the label Hydrocodone. Confusion surrounded her head as she tried to recount where the bottle came from. Didn't I flush them down the toilet? Cate hands were shaky. She hated feeling fragmented. The last 24 hours were a blur, and her head was pounding.

"Smokey is getting antsy!" Hunter hollered down the hallway.

He frightened Cate as she placed the pills in her suitcase under her clothes. I can't let Hunter find these. Cate mumbled to herself.

"Everything OK? You look like you have seen a ghost." Hunter verbalized.

"Yes, I'm ready!"

Hunter poked his index finger into the steel cage to scratch under Smokey's chin. "I think he likes me." Hunter's wide smile enhanced his deep adorable dimples. "Let me carry your suitcase."

On the drive back, Hunter couldn't help but experience serenity. A familiar love song played on the radio. Cate's blonde hair adorned across her shoulders, light as corn silk. Hunter was delighted to have Smokey as well. Growing up Hunter had a few beautiful cats that he tried to protect from Stan's wrath. If nothing else as to alert him when the old stairs would creak from his 6'4 frame coming downstairs.

"Smokey reminds me of my little tuxedo kitten — so cute...." Hunter's happiness quickly changed to sorrow as he teared up.

"Hunter, what's wrong?" Cate pressed.

"Hey Lisa!" One of the neighborhood boys shouted. "Why don't you get a dog? Cats are sneaky and stupid. You better keep the cat inside or something might happen."

The next day after school Lisa was strategically moving down the alley to avoid being seen by Stan and the boys. As Lisa ran up the hill in the backyard, she saw a tiny shape swinging by a yellow rope on the clothesline. Walking slowly toward it she could see it was her tuxedo kitten, tongue sticking out and neck broken. Screaming, she ran into the back door to retrieve some scissors. But it was obviously too late. Heartbroken, Lisa buried her kitten in the garden, hating the boys even more. Promising to protect. To survive.

At least he could keep Smokey safe. Hunter used his flannel shirt sleeve to wipe away his tears. "I will tell you about it sometime." He tried to muster up some confidence.

Back at the house Hunter changed the bed sheets and washed some towels. He left some on the dresser in his room for Cate who was showering. Smokey was exploring the house and basement, too curious to eat. Hunter took his blanket and pillow to make a bed on the couch. He didn't want to push Cate.

"Are you hungry?" Cate said. "I'm starving."

"What do you like? I have potatoes, steak…"

Cate cut him off. "I will cook. You relax."

She was flying around the kitchen in Hunter's robe. Smokey curled up in a ball on the couch. Everything was perfect.

Hunter settled down to work for a while. He was hoping with Cate and Smokey there his words would come easier. After some time, the house was filled with a wonderful aroma. Garlic and Italian spices waft up Hunter's nose and reminded him of family dinner at Susie's parents' house that always included a full spread of pasta dishes. Susie was Italian and had the temper to go along with it.

"I hope you're hungry. Spaghetti and meatballs with a side salad." Cate announced as she continued to set the table.

"This looks amazing, Cate." Hunter exclaimed as he pulled her chair out to help her get seated. Hunter could tell Cate had exerted herself too hard. She was sweating and her cheeks were flushed.

"Have a seat. Let's relax. What plans do you have tomorrow, Cate?"

"Well, I know you need to get some work done so, I thought I could go to the market and pick up some food. You don't have much food." Cate chuckled.

"Well, I'm a bachelor, what do you expect. But I don't want you to push yourself. You had a traumatic experience. You need your rest. I can go to the market."

"I don't need to be coddled. I'm fine Hunter."

Stubborn woman! Hunter thought to himself.

After dinner, Hunter cleared the dishes and gave Smokey his dinner. Cate's knees were drawn tightly to her chest while she stared off into space. What was going on in her beautiful mind? It wasn't going to be easy to penetrate those walls.

"After dinner drink?" Hunter offered with two glasses in his hands.

"Yes, please. So, what do we do about this whole situation?"

Hunter drank his drink slowly staring at the ice cubes as if they had the magical answer to Cate's question. "We wait." Hunter spoke.

"We wait?" Cate repeated.

"This person is a creature of habit, I bet. In his mind you wronged him. So, he will be on the lookout for both of us. He is a predator, but we will be ready for him."

"Ready for him!" Cate said in disbelief.

"We need to have a plan of action. To protect us and our homes."

"Sounds good, what do you have in mind?"

Hunter topped off his glass. "I will think of something. We're in this together. We will bring him down." Hunter reassured Cate.

Smokey jumped up and circled Hunter's lap, massaging his thighs with his big catcher's mitt paws. Hunter stroked his golden furry coat and rubbed his belly.

"Well, it looks like Smokey trusts you." Cate smiled. "Animals will not expose their belly unless they trust you. So, Hunter, tell me what happened to your tuxedo kitten." Cate crossed her long shapely legs and turned towards Hunter.

He reached across her to grab a smoke, something he did when he was stalling or nervous. But he quickly changed his mind when he saw Cate's disapproval.

"OK, I will tell a story, but only if you do too." Hunter guzzled his brown concoction drawing the liquid courage he needed.

"Deal!" Cate exclaimed. "You are first."

"When I was young. I wanted to be one of the guys. But the neighborhood boys I grew up with were bullies and cruel. They would call me names like "lesbo" and "he she." The boys saw that I was getting stronger, and they tried to get me back by whatever means possible. When I came home from school one day, I found my kitten swinging, hanged on a clothesline. At that point things changed. My rage and grief merged into one. I've spent my entire life trying to separate them, Cate. I don't know if it's possible." Hunter continued to stroke Smokey.

The lines on Cate's forehead were deep and noticeable. She sensed he was holding back something, but she decided to let it go.

"Hunter I'm sorry that you experienced that. That's horrible. Now I know why you're so in tune with Smokey." Cate extended her hand to find Hunter's.

"Don't be sorry. No point in that. I'm okay." There was so much more to his awful story, but he could only give small doses at this point. "Your turn."

Cate ran her long fingers through her silky blonde hair, adjusted her clothes and took a long hard gulp of her drink.

"When Michael was young, I was a terrible parent. One good thing for someone who wants to be an absent parent is a 24-hour a day job and Edward had one. Gwen was home with him all day. Anyway, I found my birth father, before my transition, and he asked me to come see him when he was dying. Edward spent his last weeks with him. My father helped me to understand why they gave me up. It was amazing. And while I was visiting him, Edward would help give him his pills. He had stage four lung cancer.

"Anyhow, Edward started stealing his pills and taking them. Long story short, everything fell apart, my father died, and I became addicted to pain killers. Happy?" Cate took another sip and looked away.

Hunter knew that the story was a little lopsided, but he knew he had to go slow with her.

"That's so much to deal with, Cate." Hunter had to tread lightly. "Were you able to shake off the addiction?"

"I went into treatment twice and now I'm fine." Cate tapped her foot incessantly. She always did when she was lying.

"I'm tired, Hunter. All this getting to know you stuff wears me out." Cate couldn't wait to get out of the room. "I feel shaky."

"Of course." Hunter stood up. "Can Smokey stay out here with me?"

Cate was weary. "Yes. Good night, Hunter."

"Good night, Cate."

Cate woke up in a panic glued to the sweaty sheets. Her mind was racing, and her skin was ice cold. She had gone through withdrawal many times, but this was rougher; something else was still travelling in her blood stream. As she sat on the edge of the bed and tried to gather herself, the events of the other night played out in her mind in bits and pieces. On her way to the concert, she was starting to get a buzz from drinking at the house. She had forgotten about digging in her purse and finding a few white pills with dirt and fuzz on them in the bottom. She had popped them without thinking.

Walking into the entrance, Cate already felt the effect of the pills she had taken earlier. Faceless people and lights were blending. A man came up to her and asked if she wanted a drink. When she said "yes," the man assumed that she wanted him to watch the concert with her. After the second beer everything was black until Hunter rescued her. The mysterious man had no face yet.

I was drugged. Cate said to herself. And I was already high.

She needed some pills now. Cate's mind went into a frenzied state. Where had she hidden them? She checked her purse, then tore apart her suitcase and reclaimed them. She was grateful Hunter brought in some water before he went to bed. Cate took the pills and hid them back in her suitcase. She wanted to lie back down and wait for sunrise.

The morning sun peeked through the window, illuminating Hunter's dusty hardwood floors. A giant yellow piece of butterscotch candy, that's how Hunter described the sun as a child to his grandmother. She always had a glass bowl of candies on the coffee table.

He loved going over to her house with the whole house smelling of freshly baked cinnamon rolls. She would make extra, and Lisa and she would go down under the bridge to give homeless people breakfast. When they returned home, grandma would play the piano as Lisa lay on the floor and watched her two different colored shoes pumping the pedals. The yellow shoe had a hole cut out of the center, and her red shoe a hole in the exact spot where her bunions protruded out. She was Hunter's only grandparent.

Smokey sprang up next to Hunter on the couch. He ambled to the bathroom. It was getting easier to walk now. The soft tissue was healing, and the nerve endings generated a new sensation. Soft fur nudged gently against Hunter's hairy legs. Smokey scaped his claws against Cate's door and pushed it open a little further. Hunter popped his head inside. Cate was sleeping peacefully on her back.

Time has been good to her. Hunter thought to himself. The rays of sunlight accentuated her long flower-like eyelashes. It had been two days since Stan attacked Cate. Her bruises were dark, a necklace of purple, yellow, and black fingerprints around her neck. After all that she had been through, Hunter wanted her to sleep. Out in the kitchen Smokey did his dance and called for his breakfast. Hunter started the coffee and jumped in the shower.

Smokey was sitting on the edge of the bathtub playfully swatting at the shower curtain. Hunter let the water cover his head, trying to contain his anger at Stan. He was going to make him pay for all the pain he has caused. Smokey peeked his head around the shower curtain to see what Hunter was doing. It reminded him of Cate, safe and asleep. Hunter would go to the market and let Cate sleep. As he was toweling off, he realized his clothes were in the room with Cate.

Hunter wrapped the towel around his waist and quietly creaked the door open. She didn't move, but Smokey snuggled in with her. Before Hunter left, he wrote a note for Cate. Went to the market. Coffee is made. Be back soon.

The clean fall air cleared Hunter's head. A faint trace of Cate's perfume lingered in his truck. Their attraction was more than physical. She was a perfect mix of what Hunter needed — acceptance and passion. Cate's drug abuse was a possible red flag, but it seemed it was in the past. And he was in no place to judge.

Hunter knew addiction could devour you from the inside out, slowly consuming you whole. Hunter wrote about pain and abuse, but he hoped to get to the point where he could write about healing and prosperity. Maybe he could even experience it firsthand.

Inside the store, Hunter picked up a new bottle of scotch and a few things for dinner. He purchased Smokey a black collar with silver spikes on it and on impulse, some mouse toys with cat nip inside. As he paid for his groceries, he rounded up two fresh sunflowers from the teaser display by the register.

Now remember, Lisa, sunflowers need space to grow. Place the seeds in deep and spread them apart a couple inches. This row is yours which means you take care of it. If it's dry, you water it. Pull all the weeds and try to keep the animals and insects away.

Hunter's father's love language was his flower garden and growing tomatoes and corn. He would always tell me to stop by and pick up some fruits and vegetables. I miss these moments, Hunter thought to himself.

Hunter carefully carried the large, yellow blooms to bring to Cate. On the way home, he saw passed some homeless people fighting over garbage in the dumpster. People are primal just like animals. Survival of the fittest. Hunter wanted to believe in humanity but sometimes it was difficult. For today, he would work this afternoon and have a nice dinner. No expectations, just a willingness and openness to listen, whatever Cate was ready to share.

Back at Hunter's, Cate was trying to get out of bed. Her whole body ached. Smokey was sleeping at the edge of the bed. Cate shuffled out to the kitchen and filled her glass up with water. She was angry with herself for taking the pills. On the kitchen table she saw a note. She smiled and made her some coffee.

Hunter is considerate, she thought to herself. She didn't want to screw things up. Be careful, Cate! She knew she was a master at self-sabotage, a defense mechanism learned in the foster care system. When someone tried to get close, she would push them away before they could leave. In her world, adults abandoned you. So, she beat them to the punch.

Edward! Why are you playing with those dolls? What is wrong with you? We have other children here who have a chance at life. All you're doing is confusing them. Go into the room with the boys and play cowboys and Indians like a normal boy.

Edward, what are you wearing? Take those off at once!? Those are girls' clothes!

Edward, you must fit in. Edward, what's wrong with you!?

Smokey perched on the windowsill, sunning. The cat jumped down when he heard the keys jingling in the lock. Cate needed a few more minutes to collect herself so she went back into the bedroom to get dressed.

Hunter was greeted at the front door by two large blue cat eyes staring at him.

"Well, hello Smokey," Hunter said as he patted him on the head. "Where is your mom?"

"I'm here," Cate chimed in. "Let me help you."

"You're a guest. I have it." Hunter went past Cate and set the bags in the kitchen on the counter.

"Hunter, I would rather help. I'm not used to being waited on." Cate spoke gently.

"By all means! After you..." Hunter handed her a jar.

"Yes. I will put them all away." She began to tuck the groceries neatly into their shelves. "So... last night I was starting to have flashbacks of the concert."

"Really? That's good." Hunter replied shoving his hands in his pockets.

"I remember a man, but I can't see his face. He brought me a beer. I was listening to music, then I blacked out."

"Do you remember me pulling you out of his car?"

"Bits and pieces, it's all blurred together. I think he drugged me." Cate's hand shook as she pushed her hair back from her face. "I'm not sure what to do." Cate sounded exasperated. "Should I file a police report?"

Hunter sat at the kitchen table. He had to think fast. He didn't want to divulge to Cate that he knew who the faceless man was. Not yet.... He wanted to take care of Stan on his own, one-on-one.

"Cate. It's been a couple days. If you were going to file a report it should have been that night. Trans people don't have much credibility with the police. We are not their number one priority." Hunter hated that he wasn't being completely truthful. And he looked uncomfortable, tapping his fingers on the table. He hoped Cate couldn't sense it.

"So, I sit around and do nothing? I still have bruises and I'm sure some of the drug is still in my system. You don't think they would believe me? I thought you would support me. I guess I was wrong." Cate went out the back door and sat on the deck.

Hunter picked up the sunflowers and brought them outside. "Here, I wanted to give these to you." Hunter hoped this would smooth things over for now.

Cate wanted to be angry at Hunter, but she gave in. "Thank you. They are beautiful."

"The flowers would make a lovely center piece at the dinner table tonight. I need to work for a while, but I want to cook for you." Hunter flashed his impish grin.

"That would be nice. I'm going to lie back down with Smokey. My head is throbbing." Cate headed back inside with her flowers.

Hunter stayed on the deck a little longer taking in the midmorning sun and air. He wasn't happy about telling Cate half-truths, but it was for her own protection. Stan was dangerous. Their parents were aware how dangerous he was, but the police never were able to solve the problem. A cloak and dagger mission was the only way.

The first sign of trouble for Stan was at eleven years old. He stole a car and picked up some friends. They ended up flipping the car and one of the passengers broke his leg – a compound fracture. The kid's parents filed a lawsuit against Hunter's family. From there it just went downhill. Stan was expelled from school for constant fighting, drugs, and petty theft.

It eventually split the family apart. No matter what he did or said, Lisa's mother coddled Stan. The truth is she felt responsible for his behavior. Maybe if she had loved him more, was a stay-at-home mom instead of working. But some people are born evil. Stan was a bad seed.

Their youngest sister had the right idea. She left as soon as she had the opportunity, and went as far as she could go, to the east coast. To this day, Hunter wondered how she was doing, and wished he had been able to go with her. There was more than one way to survive, that's for sure.

CHAPTER 9

Cate tossed and turned in the bedroom. Smokey flicked his tail as he settled and resettled next to her, hoping he could curl up for the night.

The sunflowers' bright yellow pedals mesmerized her. An intricate and wild beauty. Cate touched her aching neck, fingering the fresh lumps and deep contusions. She wanted to enjoy this moment with the picturesque flowers and Smokey finally showing her some attention. But Hunter's relationship with Smokey was so effortless and fluid, already better than hers. Feelings are so irrational, Cate thought to herself. Fear vibrated through her. She had lost Michael; would she lose Smokey? He placed his paw gently on her arm until she fell back asleep.

In the next room, Hunter ideas flowed onto the paper. The sunflowers brought back memories, so many colors Hunter had forgotten. As a young girl, Hunter would sit outside in the dirt playing marbles while mom would hang the clothes out to dry. The big cat eye was her favorite marble. You could hold it up to the light and the colors were frozen like an image of a sandbar in the river. Lisa would image herself inside the cat eye developing x-ray vision to escape her present existence and spring forward to a new one. That is, when she wasn't tending the garden. Moments of peace.

Enough daydreaming for now, Hunter said to himself. I need to get dinner started. He wanted tonight to be special. Their lovemaking replayed in his mind. Ivory skin flushed against his, Cate's delicate ruby lips hungerly searching for him, their bodies together like branches on a tree. But it was going to be difficult to get back to being intimate. Hunter wanted to but Cate was not ready. He would wait patiently and let things unfold naturally.

A clicking sound diverted Hunter out of his head. Across the hardwood floor, Smokey's long nails announced his arrival.

"Do we need to cut your claws? How are you going to be able to sneak up on your prey like that? You might as well wear a bell on your collar." Hunter knelt and stroked his shiny fur. Hunter gave Smokey some food and began chopping vegetables.

Cate sat on the bed staring out the window. Her dreams were vivid and wild. She was running in a forest at night. He was chasing her, he was close... his whiskey breath hot on the back of her neck. He jabbed her with a syringe. Then she woke up tied to a chair in an abandon house, with a sinking feeling that she would never be free again.

Her suitcase was partially zipped, but the bottle cap was exposed. The pills had a magnetic pull.

"Just one. No big deal." Cate said out loud.

"Cate," Hunter called as he opened the door.

The door creaking open startled Cate as the pill rolled out of her hand and spun under the bed.

"You OK, Cate? You lose something?"

"I dropped my contact." Cate trailed off as she looked under the bed past the dust bunnies to find the pill.

"Let me help!" Hunter moved forward.

"I don't need your help!" Cate snapped back. "Please don't fuss over me!"

"OK... Dinner is ready. Take your time." Hunter closed the door.

The pill had dust and dirt on it, but she didn't care. It was bitter going down and by the time it reached her stomach the guilt devoured and overcame her.

Hunter didn't deserve to be treated that way. He'll leave and not want anything to do with me again. Cate's legs could barely support her.

Hunter was pulling food out of the oven and Smokey was in the window watching. His movements were choppy and abrupt.

"Can I help set the table?" Cate said sheepishly.

"The plates are above the stove." Hunter replied.

Cate set the plates down and placed her head on his broad shoulders and wrapped her arms around his V-shaped waist. "I'm sorry.... I'm not used to co-habitation." Cate confessed.

"Don't be sorry. Pour us a drink." Hunter said, finally smiling.

"Dinner smells wonderful." Cate mixed their cocktails and breathed a sigh of relief.

Hunter served the food in generous portions and lit a scented candle as the center piece. Some bluesy music was playing in the background as Hunter dimmed the lights.

The pill was starting to take effect, mixed with the mellowing scotch. Cate decided to eat slowly as to not ruin her light buzz.

"How are you healing up, Cate?" Hunter inquired.

"Slowly. The bruises are fading, and the cuts are going away. I'm having some nightmares." Cate pushed her food around with her fork.

"Oh... do you want to talk about them?"

Cate sat back in her chair and took a sip. Maybe it would help. "I'm running in pitch black woods, and I'm cold, and the trees are cutting me, but I must keep going. I try to be quiet. But everywhere I run, there are cracking and breaking sounds. Then, I hear footsteps coming up behind me, breath on the back of my neck. The faster I run the darker it gets, and the footsteps come closer and closer. I make the mistake of looking back as I ran a tree root catches my foot and I tumble hard into the dirt. Then he pushes me down. He injects a shot in my neck that's all I remember until I wake up tied to a chair. I escape again, but it all starts again... and then I realize this is what he wants - the continual chase. Horrible. What do you think it means?"

Hunter places his fork and knife on his plate. "At least this — it represents the attack and your fear of it happening again. It might mean more, but that's for you to find." Hunter reached his hand out to touch Cate. "We will get through this together."

"You can't be with me every moment. I need to go back to work on Monday."

"I know. But we will figure this out. I promise." Hunter raised his glass with self-assurance.

"Why don't we go on the patio with our drinks. We can clean up later. It's a beautiful evening."

Cate needed some air. The drinks were going straight to her head, as she held on to the chair to conceal her intoxication. "A full moon. It's lovely."

Hunter traces Cate's face and kissed her lips softly. "Not as lovely as you in the moonlight."

Cate kissed him back as a primal ache surged throughout her limbs. Then she pulled away. "Hunter, I'm not – I have to go home tomorrow."

Hunter tried to hide his disappointment. "OK, but can you consider the idea of us being together?"

Cate bit her lower lip and stared at the moon. "I am attracted to you, Hunter."

"But?"

"My focus right now needs to be on my work. What happened the other night really frightened me. I don't know who I can trust." Cate finished her drink.

"If you don't trust me, then why are you here?"

"Can we go in? I'm a bit chilly." Cate stood up.

Both remained silent as they cleared off the dinner table and fed scraps to Smokey. The tension was brutal.

"I don't want things to be awkward. Can't we just listen to some more music and talk?" Cate proposed.

Hunter nodded and let Smokey escort them to the sitting room. Cate sat close to Hunter while Smokey napped on the arm of the couch.

"When did you realize you were trans?" Hunter blurted out.

The random question caught Cate off guard, but the drinks and the pill made it seem natural to share. "I've always known at some level. It was more than dressing up in my girls' clothes and make up. I wanted to live my truth. Edward was never me."

"For me, Lisa and Hunter are intertwined. I tried to shut the door on Lisa and never look back. She kept popping up like an unwanted guest. I must learn from her so I can live with no regret as Hunter. Being Lisa and everything I went through made me a better man."

Cate shook her head. "When I started taking hormones it was like a weight lifted and I could see clearly for the first time– I was the woman I was meant to be. Edward was so foreign. After my bottom surgery I felt reborn. It was worth all the time, pain, and money. But you understand – I guess you also lost things in the process."

"Those who genuinely want to be in our world will try. It's that simple." Hunter unconsciously reached for a cigarette.

Cate seized them and shook her finger in a disconcerting manner, scolding Hunter like a schoolchild. "Cigarettes killed my father. I'm looking out for you." She placed them in her pocket and settled back against him. "We leave people we love behind when we transition. My son is married and has a daughter that I have never seen. 'I don't want your depraved lifestyle corrupting my daughter!' That's what he said. Depraved lifestyle! His ignorance It breaks my heart. Wow, I'm talking too much." Cate stood up and refilled her drink.

Smokey jumped inside a cardboard box under the coffee table. Cate waved at him, a little drunkenly. "Hey! Smokey, get out of there. Pictures! May I look?"

"Oh, those are nothing." Hunter shook his head no, but Cate was already rummaging through them.

"Is this you? Before your transition?" Cate asked.

"Yes, it's painful to look at sometimes." Hunter admitted.

"Who is this stunning woman?" Cate shouted.

"Susie." Hunter was thankful for his drink to calm his nerves.

"She is gorgeous. Tell me about her."

"Not much to tell." Hunter picked up Smokey and placed him on his lap unintentionally creating a barrier between Cate and him.

"Hunter, I bared my soul to you. It's only fair." Cate expressed wringing her hands together.

Cate isn't being completely honest, Hunter thought, but he wanted to gain her trust.

"We met at a friend's birthday party. I was already trying to figure out about transitioning but I didn't have the courage or resources for it. My friends said I was a lesbian, and I just needed a good woman. Anyway, it was mostly great until she decided I cheated. I was struggling, drinking to much, I got angry a lot. Susie sat me down and demanded the truth — 'Who are you seeing behind my back!?' That's when I told her that I was going to start testosterone. It totally blindsided her. We had been together for seven years. I always felt if she really knew me it would be self-explanatory. So, she left. I can't say that I blame her. Susie wanted to be with a woman." Hunter averted his eyes from Cate's blistering stare.

"I understand about havoc and devastation in relationships. Gwen and Michael blame me for every misfortune in their life." Cate sighed.

"Cate, do you really have to go home tomorrow? I've loved our time together. Not the circumstances, but I'm glad you're here. Can you stay?"

"No. I must go back to work. There's this work spy, Jane, she watches me like a hawk and reports anything she finds suspicious. The funny thing is she is married and chases any man in a white coat. Catches them, too. The hypocrisy is nauseating."

"Well, you will go back and prove her wrong." Hunter clapped his hands together.

"It's getting late. I'm going to bed." Cate walked toward the bedroom but turned around. She blushed as she played with her buttons on her shirt. "Are you coming?"

Hunter placed his glass on the table and moved Smokey off his lap. "Come on, boy." Smokey jumped down and followed him to the bedroom. The light from the moon illuminated Cate's silhouette under the covers she was already in bed. Hunter removed his boots and jeans and crawled in, pressing his chiseled body against her. Smokey sprung up on the pillow, purring.

Cate's smooth skin and the smell of her sent a jolt of desire and longing through Hunter. But the timing was off, and Hunter didn't want to cross the line. This is where he wanted to be. I can wait, he thought, as he drifted off to sleep.

The next morning Smokey used Hunter's bladder as a launching pad to wake him up. He rushed to the bathroom with Smokey right behind him. "Smokey, I guess you're hungry, right boy?" Hunter scratched under his chin, Smokey's favorite spot.

Hunter started the coffee pot. He sat at the kitchen table and opened the window for Smokey to watch and cackle at the birds when a wave of sadness overwhelmed him. Cate was going home today with Smokey. Hunter wasn't ready to be alone again. Hopefully, they would be back soon.

Cate finally woke up, rested and cheerful. "Good morning, Hunter, the coffee smells wonderful!" Cate openly admired his rock-hard leg muscles and his hairy legs. She had found it hard, waiting for him to sleep instead of kissing him.

Hunter laughed. "I need my pants. I will be right back." In the bedroom he bobbled around to put his jeans on. "Where are those socks?" Hunter muttered. He saw one of his black socks under the bed, bending down he saw a white pill.

Is this an aspirin? Hunter pinched the circular tablet between his fingers.

"Hunter, your coffee is getting cold." Cate bellowed from the other room.

He hid the pill in his dresser drawer and returned to the kitchen. "Are you hungry?"

"I can eat at home. I'm going to shower and then we can go if that's OK with you."

"Sure." Hunter tried to not have his voice reflect his true feelings. "Towels are in the closet." The pill was bothering him. So, he went into the bedroom to investigate. Cate's suitcase was partially open. He heard the water in the shower.

It wasn't in his nature to snoop but something didn't feel right. He unzipped the suitcase the rest of the way. Clothes, toothbrush, and hygiene products were on top. There was a side zipper that caught his eye.

"Hunter! Can you bring me a towel?"

He zipped the suitcase back up this wasn't the time to look too obviously. Hunter opened the bathroom door and placed the towel on the sink. In the mirror Cate's shape flowed like a breeze in the fall trees. He watched the soap fall off her body as she rinsed her long golden hair. Smokey ran past him and leaped up on the toilet.

"Did you get a good look?" Cate said laughing as she toweled her goddess like curls.

"I don't know what you mean," Hunter said bashfully.

"It's not like you haven't seen me before." Cate lowered her towel and playfully started dressing slowly.

Two can play this game. Hunter thought. Taking his shirt off he went to the closet and retrieved a fresh shirt. In front of the mirror, he ran his fingers through his thick lion's mane, making sure he flexed his pectoral muscles. Cate who was trying not to stare but he could see her watching in the mirror. Hunter finished dressing leisurely.

"I will take your suitcase out to my truck." Did she have drugs in the side compartment? In the truck on the floorboard Hunter saw Smokey's black spiked collar. It must have fallen out of the bag.

Cate came out of the bedroom with her sunflowers. "I never told you thank you. They are gorgeous. I'm taking them with me."

"Smokey, come here boy." Hunter situated the spiked collar on him.

Cate was laughing hard and loud. "He hates it!" Smokey was using his back-rabbit legs to dig under the collar to squeeze it off his head. "Don't worry. He will get used to it. Smokey thanks you."

"Are you ready to go?"

"Yes, here are your cigarettes. Smoke only a few please."

"I will get Smokey."

The disappointment in his voice hurt Cate's heart. "I have an idea this week is going to be busy and I'm working some double shifts to catch up. Would you watch Smokey? I don't want him to be alone for that long."

Hunter's face lit up. "Really? I mean are you sure?"

"I'm positive. He likes you."

"When will you come to see him? Hunter asked.

"Soon! You have my baby!" Cate smirked.

"He will be my writing buddy. I hope you're letting me keep him so you can come over whenever you please?" Hunter beamed with mischief.

"Maybe… Hey, thank you for everything. I would not have been able to stay alone." Cate's voiced cracked her head slumped forward hiding the fear in her face.

"Hey," Hunter twirled her around to face him. "If you need me, I'm here. I want you to feel safe." Hunter mounted his arms around Cate gently.

Cate fell into his chest his strong heart beating in accord with hers. His smell was exhilarating. She knew that it was too late. They were falling in love.

HUNTER

CHAPTER 10

Over the next few weeks Hunter and Smokey developed a comfortable routine. He would get up in the morning, have coffee and feed his purring companion before his shower, and then have breakfast. Then he would spend the day writing and working on house projects. His memoir kept veering into fiction, a place where he could imagine all kinds of ways to enact revenge on Stan.

Cate came over on the weekends to play with Smokey and spend time with Hunter. He kept reminding himself to be patient, that they were getting closer. Of course, she never said, but he could sense their relationship was deeper. Her work seemed to be going OK. Hunter kept putting off research on the numbers printed on the white pill in the drawer. Things were going so well.

If Cate was lying to him about her drug use, he didn't know what he would do. Hunter knew too many friends and acquaintances killed by their addiction, and of course, there was his own mother. Hunter was worried. But before he confronted her, he wanted to take her on a little trip. And he filtered his angst into his writing, getting closer to a plan to destroy his brother.

He would do it after their trip, he decided, as he packed an overnight bag. "You be a good boy, Smokey. We won't be gone long." Hunter kissed him on his cold nose and went out the front door. He headed over to get Cate.

Hunter was taking Cate to his father's old cabin an hour up north. His cousin helped with the upkeep and Hunter shared expenses from his inheritance. Robert's dad, Hunter's uncle, had been a gifted artist. Cousin Robert and Lisa would watch him paint for hours in his basement, sneaking a beer as the three of them talked away from his overbearing wife's eagle eye. She could spot alcohol a mile away. When she was young her father would drink up all the money. They had to steal from the neighbor's gardens to put food on the table.

Hunter's uncle would leave six packs out the backdoor. Lisa and Robert would grab him a beer when they would go upstairs for a soda. They didn't care. It was a game to them. He gave them candy and the radio would play oldies music. He was a kind man who died too soon.

When Hunter's father passed, he promised to take care of the cabin, a sanctuary for fishing, and swimming, surrounded by beautiful gardens. Winter was magical, too. The frozen lake cracked eerily all night, glimmering in the moonlight. There was plenty of wildlife. Cate will love it up there.

Hunter finally made it to Cate's, honking his horn even though she was expecting him. After a few minutes he tried to call her, no answer. He went up to the door and rang her doorbell.

"Cate… it's me! Are you here?"

Finally, the door opened. "Sorry, let me get my bag."

Hunter held the door open; the house was in ruins. Clothes on the floor and furniture. Empty take out containers on the coffee table. Beer bottles on the floor.

"Is everything OK, Cate?"

"I'm fine." Cate said as she put her sunglasses on.

Hunter fetched her bag and reluctantly went inside. "Did you have a rough week?" Hunter probed.

"You could say that. Jane is like a dog on a bone waiting for me to mess up. There is a promotion coming up and she wants it." Cate exhaled.

"Where are we going? This isn't the way to your house."

"I have a surprise for you. Sit back and enjoy the ride." Hunter turned up the radio and savored the moment. He thought Cate might say more, and she hated being pushed. If he cornered her when she wasn't ready Cate would fight or grow cold. Hunter didn't want either to happen.

On the drive over fall became winter as they moved up into the mountains. The trees were bare and if you looked close enough resembled thick fingers extending for the clouds. With the colorful leaves already fallen you could see for miles. The cool crisp air had a cleansing effect.

Hunter was grateful for the chance for them to recharge their batteries. Susie was texting him, wanting to see him. He didn't want to go, but she had a way of triggering Hunter, and she would use it if she could. Cate would blow a gasket if she knew, but hadn't he said he didn't want to be with Susie? A new relationship can be a gray area difficult to steer through.

"Are we almost there?" Cate hung her hand out the window.

"Yes, a mile or two." Hunter placed his hand on Cate's inner thigh for reassurance.

The gravel road leading to the cabin was covered with a white blanket of snow. Deer tracks crossed the road, and Hunter saw Robert's Ford parked by the porch.

Robert was one of Hunter's few family members that accepted his transition. As he put it, "I never saw you as Lisa."

"Hunter!" Robert yelled, "How the hell are you?" Robert embraced him in a bear hug.

"Robbie, you look great! How is your family?"

"Everyone is fine. Kids are growing like weeds." Robert replied.

"This is my girl, Cate - don't bear hug her." Hunter chuckled. "Cate, this is my cousin Robert. We look after this place."

"You must be cold. The fireplace is going! Come on in." Robert yelled over his shoulder as he went into the cabin.

"My dad's baseball trophies! You put them in a glass case?" Hunter shouted with enthusiasm as he lowered their bags on the floor. "Cate, come on in!" Hunter took her hand. "Have a look around."

"Your dad could have gone somewhere after playing college ball. But both of our dads were drafted." Robert rubbed the glass case with a towel.

"This place is cozy." Cate said.

"Hunter, I have something for you." Robert went behind the kitchen counter and pulled out a stand with a cloak covering it. "Go ahead! Have a look."

"Cate, do the honors." She enclosed her long-manicured nails around the cloak and lifted delicately.

"Robert! Your dad's painting!" Hunter roared.

"After he died, my sister and I went through his paintings in the basement. I remember the day he painted it. This was your favorite - the ocean striking the rocks."

"So powerful." Cate commented.

Hunter ran his fingers over the brush strokes on the canvas. "Now, Lisa, grab me a beer and I will show you how to paint hands. They are the most difficult." Hunter could almost hear his voice now.

Fighting back the tears, Hunter moved away. "Robert, the place looks amazing. At least stay for dinner before you head back."

"If your lady friend doesn't mind. I wouldn't want to intrude."

"We would love to have you!" Cate chimed in.

"All right it's settled then. I can go pick up some groceries for you. How long are you staying?" Robert asked.

"Two days. We have a critter to get home to." Hunter smirked.

"Let me guess - a cat." Robert grinned.

"You know me well." Hunter laughed. "Let me write a list for you. We can catch up at dinner."

"You two have a unique relationship," Cate observed as they unpacked.

"Yes, he and my father stood by me through everything. We don't stay in touch much but when we get together it's so comforting to pick up right where we left off."

"I'm envious. I lost everything when I transitioned." Cate began to feel sorry for herself.

Hunter rotated Cate toward him. "I'm sorry you had to experience that. Just know I want to be your family now." He leaned in and parted his lips to gently kiss Cate.

She kissed him back passionately, but part of her still held back. She had been using again, and the guilt was shrouded in her chest.

"The lake is out front. Come take a look." Hunter glowed like a schoolboy sharing his favorite fishing spots and bringing her at last to the dormant garden beds. "In the spring my dad would plant his flowers, corn, and tomatoes here. I would help him pick the vegetables and tend to the flowers. "Hunter's face crumpled suddenly.

"Are you OK?" Cate touched his shoulder.

"My dad's ashes are in this garden. On his deathbed, he asked." That moment played again in his mind.

Hunter, I know what you're going to say. What about your sister and Stan? Your sister is too wrapped up in her new life to care. Stan well don't bother with him. You were there with me every summer, Hunter, getting things ready for planting. So, it makes sense that you do it. I'm proud of you....

"He died in my arms. He made me promise to spread his remains here – and then he told me to honor Lisa as well as Hunter. To never forget her. It was monumental. Because of him, instead of running from Lisa, I started accepting her."

Hunter kneeled on the ground and stroked the frozen earth. Cate knelt with him, and they both sat together, silent. Cate couldn't explain but kneeling in stillness moved her.

"Robert will be back soon. Let's get warm by the fire." Cate covered his hand with hers. Hunter stomach filled with butterflies as they tried to walk in the same footprints they made coming out to the garden. Cate was frisky today and Hunter adored it.

"You two love birds enjoying the lake?" Robert chuckled as he put the bags on the table.

"I forgot how much I love this place!"

"Why don't you two catch up and I will make dinner." Cate opened the cupboard doors and found some cooking utensils.

"Grab us both a beer while I tend to the fire." Robert hollered.

"So, Robert, how are things going?" Hunter said as he cracked open two beers.

"The boys and I are going deer hunting tomorrow. Do you want to come?"

"Robert, you know better than that." Hunter took a long swig.

"I know, can't blame me for trying. Cate, when we were kids my older brother would take us hunting and Hunter would freeze up. We couldn't get him to the pull the trigger. He would say, Look at their eyes. They are such beautiful creatures. It must be his feminine side poking through." Robert chuckled.

"Robert, you know I don't like that word. It never described me." Hunter's tone became stern.

"Why, buddy? We're all made up of both sides." Robert patted Hunter's shoulder and went out to get wood.

Cate came out of the kitchen wiping her delicate hands on a towel. "Hunter, he doesn't really understand. I would shudder at the thought of being referred to as masculine."

"If he would have said Lisa, I could handle that because she is a part of me."

"Dinner is ready! We can talk later." Cate stirred the magical soup on the stovetop.

"Something smells wonderful." Robert shouted, coming back in balancing an armful of logs and another six-pack.

Cate smiled. "I'm finishing up. I hope you boys are hungry!"

"Hunter," Robert's forehead crinkled up. "Have you seen Stan?"

"No, why would you ask?"

"Well, I heard through the grapevine he is a suspect in a murder. Not that it surprises me."

"No, I haven't seen him."

"I just want you to be safe. You might want to be careful. You're a carbon copy! Let's eat!"

Soon, the three relaxed at the rustic pine table. "Cate, this is the best meal I've had in a long time. I promise – I won't tell my wife. She'll think fast food was on the menu tonight." Robert wiped his mouth showing some crooked teeth.

"The sauce is perfect, Cate!" Hunter exclaimed.

Robert grew serious again. "Listen, I wanted to give you a heads up, Hunter. Those abandoned cabins just through the woods – Cate, you can see them with the leaves gone from the trees. Anyway, some teenagers still get inside for parties — drinking, drugs, sex. The sheriff knows about it, but he would rather give tickets for expired hunting licenses. Keep an eye out. They're technically on the edge of our property. I told the sheriff in the spring I would either tear them down or make them structurally sound."

"Dad had the same problems during planting season. The kids would track all over his flowers and vegetables. He scared them off a couple times. You know my dad; his rifle was always ready."

"I remember! Pass the potatoes, Hunter. I'm sorry Cate - we are being rude. What do you do for a living? And how did my lucky cousin find you?"

"Oh, I love listening to you boys talking. If you must know I'm a nurse. I met Hunter after his surgery."

"The minute I saw her face, I was hooked!" Hunter countered.

"Well, Hunter has always had a way with the ladies," Robert joked.

"Come on, Robert." Hunter turned red.

"Really? Now I need to hear this. I'm all ears." Cate answered.

"Well, let's just say Hunter dragged me to a party once because he didn't want to go alone. He ended up dating the prettiest girl in the room." Robert claimed as he snatched the last roll.

"Was her name Susie by any chance?" Cate interrogated.

"That sounds about right," Robert nodded, surprised.

Cate glanced at Hunter and could tell by the blood rushing out of his face he wasn't comfortable. "Would you gentlemen excuse me?"

Hunter stood up from the table as she left the room. "Robert!" Hunter yelled throwing his napkin at him. "What are you doing?"

"I was just giving her some history about you."

"Well, you could have skipped that!"

In the bathroom Cate was splashing cold water on her face. Hunter will never love me I'm not a cis female. Doesn't he realize how much harder it was to become a woman? I'll never be as beautiful as Susie will be, naturally! Sure, Cate is the butterfly; Edward was a grub. But I can't compete with Susie.

Hunter was a little worried. "Cate... Robert had to go. He wanted me to thank you for dinner. Come have an after-dinner drink with me." Hunter bargained with her through the door.

The door opened and Cate came out and started to clear the table.

"Hey, I can do that later. Come sit down have a drink. Why are you crying, love?" Hunter handed her a cocktail.

"Can I ask you a question? And I want the truth. Don't sugarcoat it to spare my feelings."

"OK." Hunter stroked her back.

"I know I'm not a real woman. I'm never going to be like Susie. She is a goddess, and a cis woman. Do you wish I was her?" Cate shaded her face and swallowed hard.

"What's this, Cate?" Hunter cradled her hair. "You're a masterpiece. You created your own beauty. I see you Cate. I see you."

"You beautiful man." Cate whispered inches from Hunter's mouth. Seducing him with her breath. Their mouths became intwined searching hungrily for this passion to be extinguished.

Hunter's artistic hands unbuttoned her blouse as he kissed her collar bone. Cate ran her fingers through Hunter's thick curly hair pressing her skin into him. Cate helped Hunter rip his t-shirt off exposing his rippling biceps. She kissed his pecks and ran her nails down his warrior body. Hunter moaned and kissed her deeper. They both fumbled to undo Hunter's belt buckle. Cate started rubbing his penis as his fully healed manhood rose to attention.

Cate fingered the scar on his leg where his new penis had been harvested and pulled his underwear down. "I want you inside me." Cate pleaded.

Nerves were playing tennis in his stomach. Hunter picked Cate up with ease and led her into the bedroom. Laying her down gently on the bed, he removed the rest of her clothes, kissing her voluptuous body. Cate interlaced her long ballerina like legs around Hunter's V-shaped hips and powerful back.

He inserted himself gently into Cate as she tightened her grip and kissed his neck. They fit together perfectly in harmony. Colors and vivid shapes consumed their heads as they tangled and coiled into each other.

Cate's erratic breath sent his head flying. He wanted to wrap up inside her away from the world holding on to this precious and beautiful moment. Her nails dug deep in his back as she let out a primal cry. Hunter blasted with the buildup in his stomach when he kissed her his body convulsed with her and jerked fiercely.

As they lay there, spent, and sweaty. Cate yearned to stay close for the first time in a long time. Her only fear was now only that she might lose Hunter. This newfound realization sent ice running through her veins. She was in deep. There was no turning back.

Hunter swam in a bay of completeness. For the first time he could use his body the way he always wanted to.

"Hunter," Cate traced his face. "Why the tears?"

"All these years of surgeries and hormones. Praying for peace and contemplating suicide. The isolation and sneers from the outside world. Now, I can finally tell that little girl by the oak tree bargaining with God to become a boy, Lisa, you are whole."

Cate brushed her cheek against his face and kissed his tears. No more words needed to be spoken. This was a moment of triumph, and they treasured the quiet sense of wholeness each of them experienced, together.

HUNTER

CHAPTER 11

The next morning at sunrise, the birds woke Cate up. She thought about snagging a shower first. But instead, she sat on the edge of the bed and watched rays of sunlight cuddle Hunter's sleeping body, folding him up in pure perfection.

Finally, she went into the shower to indulge a few more minutes. The hot water was rejuvenating and clear. She wanted to go out into the woods and explore with Hunter today. Everything was new. Cate was content when the bathroom creaked open. She wiped off the condensation so she could see Hunter as he was using the bathroom.

Cate had hated her maleness so much that she couldn't even look at her penis when she was Edward, hated cis men's comfort with their nakedness. But something about Hunter and how natural he is was with all his masculinity appealed to her. He turned her on.

"Room for one more?" Hunter smirked opening the shower curtain.

"If you want breakfast, I need to get dressed." Cate found a clean towel and kissed his mouth.

"You do realize that I can cook." Hunter laughed.

"Yes, but I really enjoy doing it for you. So, eggs and bacon it is." Cate dressed quickly and put the coffee on. Their clothes were still in the middle of the room on the floor. Last night repeated in her head while she picked them up and stacked them neatly. She cracked open the kitchen window while she scrambled eggs. The brisk air swarmed her lungs and nose.

Hunter's painting looked so real in the morning light, and drew her in. Cate could imagine herself on the shore watching the waves crash into the rocks. She placed the painting out in the living room where it would catch more sun.

"The coffee smells good." Hunter emerged, tucking his shirt into his jeans.

"Have a seat. I'll bring you a plate."

"You're spoiling me, doll. I could get used to it." Hunter winked.

"So, what are the plans today?" Cate inquired as she slowly sipped her coffee.

"Well, I thought we could go hiking, maybe some bird watching. We can see who stayed behind for the winter."

"Wonderful idea. It's a beautiful morning!"

"Dress warm. The weather out here can be deceiving. I have my father's binoculars. We can go deep in the woods."

"Here you go." Hunter tossed a pair of warm knee-high socks to Cate.

Cate wrinkled her forehead with curiosity. "You want me to wear these?"

"Bitter cold around here. I found my old boots - you can wear them. Your dress shoes won't cut it." Hunter was a little amused at Cate's scrunched look.

"Oh, you think it's funny! Well, I might like wearing knee-high socks and outdoor boots. I might make them a permanent part of my outfit." Cate teased as she unwrapped the puffy socks.

"Can't let you do that." Hunter dangled his tree trunk arms around Cate's tiny waist squeezing her closer. "I'm quite fond of you and your dress shoes," he whispered in her ear.

His breath and closeness sent shivers down her spine. She turned around to hug him and grazed the stubble on his chiseled jaw line. Running her face across his goatee and enveloping his scent made her drunk with lust.

All the blood from Hunter's body rushed to his groin. Her alabaster skin, soft with a hint of her natural smell, caught Hunter off guard. He kissed her full lips.

"We should go. Plenty of time for that." Cate coaxed as she cupped his face.

"I will fill up the thermos with fresh coffee." Hunter suggested.

Outside it was bitterly cold, but the sun was shining, and nature was still active. Squirrels scurried around carrying acorns in their mouth to stash later in a tree.

"Look Cate, it's a red bellied woodpecker!" He handed Cate the binoculars.

"Look at the red on his head!" Cate exclaimed.

"Keep your eye out for a cardinal. They mate for life so the female will be close by."

"Let's sit by this tree and watch for them," Cate encouraged him.

Hunter motioned to a large tree stump where Cate could sit. He crouched down beside her. The steam off the coffee floated toward the sky and warmed their stomachs.

"So, you would go birdwatching with your father?" Cate asked.

"Yes, I loved it. I would imagine that I was a colorful bird and could fly away anywhere in the world soaring above the clouds." Hunter gulped his coffee.

"That's a fantastic memory!" Cate curled her lip.

"The only thing we really disagreed on was he didn't like cats because they hunt birds. I would tell him it was just instinct. So, to calm things over. I would help him build birdhouses to shelter and give the birds a safe place to go."

Cate's mind spun towards familiar jealousy. She never really had anyone in her corner. The foster care system made sure of that. Roots were unearthed at any moment. And what seemed like safe roots never turned out as she hoped.

"It's cold!" Cate sought refuge in Hunter's warm arms.

"We should keep moving; it will warm us up. Besides, I want to show you something." Hunter's bright eyes sparkled like two jewels in a treasure chest.

"See if you can spot it. It's close by." Hunter challenged Cate.

Cate began to search. She imagined what the woods would look like in the spring overgrown shrubs, tree mushrooms, maybe some wild strawberries. This treasure hunt evoked a painful memory as Edward.

Edward's whining foster brother's echoing voice intruded. 'Why does Edward get to come on the Easter egg hunt with us? He is too slow — besides he is not my real brother.'

'We can't leave him at home,' Edward's foster mom snapped. 'We need his check every month so, make it work.'

Edward had stomped on some of the eggs, blaming his bully foster brother. Also, he had eaten his chocolate bunny and blamed his cruel sister, happy to see them fighting each other and ignoring him.

The glorious feeling of vindication! Cate chuckled to herself.

"Ok, Hunter I give." Cate yelled out of breath.

"You're so close!"

"Not fair. You know these woods better than I do." Cate said with frustration.

"Look on the tree trunk, right here." Hunter pointed.

A large heart chipped carefully with a knife bearing the words Hunter Loves Cate popped out. Tears welled up in her intense eyes as she touched the simple carving.

Cate outlined her fingers over the letters admiring them. "I love it."

"I didn't do it to make you cry." Hunter assured Cate while handing her his handkerchief.

"I'm just surprised. When did you do it?" Maybe my dreams are coming true.

"I snuck out when you were in the shower. Do you have enough energy to go a little further?"

"Listen, big man just because I was a little winded earlier doesn't mean that I can't keep up with you! Where are we going?" Cate hollered over her shoulder as she pushed forward.

"That's my girl! I want to check out the abandoned cabins Robert mentioned. We might need to board them up sooner than later. I don't need a bunch of kids getting hurt or anything else they get into." Hunter took the lead. "In the summer they swim in the lake. I want you to come back with me in the spring and summer we can plant some flowers and go swimming a little further down. We could go fishing." Hunter sassed.

Cate winkled her nose up in disgust.

"What, little Edward never went fishing?" Hunter joked.

"He did. He never got past the hook worm thing."

"Well, I can teach you. The cabins are up a little further."

The first cabin was obscured by some of the trees. Cate pictured how camouflaged they would be with leaves and other vegetation in the spring.

"This needs to be repaired," Hunter stated as the doorknob fell to the snowy ground.

Cobwebs swung like vines from one corner of the room to the other. The dust was so thick you could write your name in it. Partially broken furniture was scattered across the filthy floor. Small holes at the baseboard suggested vermin chewing their way in to shelter themselves from the brutal winter.

"This place needs a woman's touch," Hunter announced.

"It needs more than that." Cate mentioned as she smacked the old couch and dust particles sailed through the air. "Maybe you and Robert could fix it up and rent it out?"

Hunter let out a big breath. "I'm not around enough to be a landlord. Besides, I'm really into my writing and don't want any distractions from this stunning young woman I'm dating." Hunter's face lit up.

"Well, if you want." Cate pushed the dirt around under her foot. "I could help decorate it. For us I mean." Cate bit her lip in anticipation. "I mean we could come up in the summer hang out around here. Fix it up. Smokey would love to wander around."

"Are you telling me that you want to stick around for a while?" Hunter poked her.

"If you'll have me. Will you?" Cate buried her head in his chest absorbing his center to calm her racing heart.

Hunter softly hugged her and ran his fingers up and down her back. "I think you already know the answer to that question."

Cate kissed him on his lips and gazed lovingly into his eyes. "I'm sorry that I broke down yesterday. I hate that part of me. I don't want to drive you away – I know it's sometimes too much…."

"Don't apologize. I don't scare easy. The other cabin is just over there. Are you ready to check it out? Then we can head back. I want to make you lunch."

Back outside, light snow began to trickle down. Covering any remnants of fall. The bare trees and white ground were eerie, but peaceful. The furthest cabin had a doorstop blocking the door.

"What's this about?" Hunter kicked the block away, and they went inside.

"There is a sleeping bag and some women's clothing." Cate stood with her hand on her hip.

"Some hygiene products and food wrappers are inside the cupboard here." Hunter added.

Beer bottles filled the overflowing trash can, along with used condoms and cigarette butts. Hunter's face contorted and the corners of his mouth narrowed.

"Those damn kids! Underage drinking and sex! I could be held responsible for their actions on my property."

"I know you're upset but hear me out for a minute. Remember when you were young, and you needed somewhere to go? Away from your parent's watchful eyes. Maybe these kids just need a haven?"

"Cate, you know that I understand that. But look at it this way what if someone was raped or hurt? Or they got drunk and drowned in the lake? Bottom line, I'm liable. I will come back tonight, since they clearly sleep here, and have a talk with them. Now how about we have some potato soup?"

"Good idea. I am cold and hungry."

They walked back in silence, enjoying the snow and the wildlife foraging for food. Cate reached for Hunter's hand as they passed back by the garden with his father's remains.

"We should start a fire." Cate proposed.

"You peel the potatoes, and I will start a fire."

As she washed the potatoes, Cate called into the living room. "I could get used to it out here. I love the contrasts."

Hunter smiled as he tended to the fire. "You sound like a writer. I loved coming out here to write and clear my head."

"I want to read your book."

"I'll share my writing someday."

Cate stopped peeling the potatoes and set down the knife. She stepped into the living room. "Did you come here with Susie?"

Hunter poked at the fire for a minute. Then he turned to Cate. "Would it bother you if I had?"

"No, you were together for quite some time." Cate wiggled her foot rapidly and her face was flushed.

"Cate, you must understand I was certain then that Susie was the one. So, we did all the things people do. We spent summers here. Susie did like to fish. When we started having tension in our relationship, we came here so I could tell her – you know. But she found my literature on hormones and reassignment surgery before I could say anything. She had been OK with my top surgery, but the idea of bottom surgery pushed her over the edge. She went back home, and I didn't hear from her for a few days. Shortly after that, I told her I wasn't changing my plans, not for anyone. So, we broke up." Hunter leaned back on the kitchen counter.

Cate took a deep breath. "Lunch will take some time. You need to get out my hair for a bit. Too much testosterone is bad for my kitchen."

Hunter grinned. "Oh, one other thing." He stopped. "You look better than she did in my boots." Hunter fetched his coat and went outside.

Cate wanted to giggle but her head was racing in circles. She was having a wonderful time with Hunter and didn't want her jealousy to ruin it. Her body was aching for a pill, and the heat from the stove made her sweat. She put the potatoes in the boiling water and went into the bathroom to take her hormone pill.

They were in her overnight bag, she found them, along with the sock and the narcotics that she kept, just in case. She filled a dixie cup with water and swallowed the demon white pill along with her hormones.

What is wrong with you, Cate? She stared hard into the mirror as if the answer were magically written in lipstick. You need to get it together. Hunter is worth it. He can't find out.

Outside Hunter lit a cigarette and walked the field where he would plant in the spring. He hoped Cate would trust him, but he understood her concern. It reminded him of his rage about Sara – and his doubts that Lisa would never get what she wanted.

A bird cawing off in the distance interrupted Hunter's memory. He needed to get back. He was hungry.

Hunter and Cate ate lunch in front of the fire. Cate seemed sleepy, so he suggested that she lay down for a bit. He poured a drink, planning what he would say to the kids, how he would convince them to stay away. He packed a backpack with some snacks, water, flashlight, and his binoculars, and put his feet up by the fire. He would be prepared, like his dad had taught him.

His body hovered, as the room was fading in and out.

"Hunter!" Cate shook him.

"It's evening! You fell asleep on the couch."

"Oh," Hunter rubbed his face and neck.

"Are you still going to check on the cabins?"

"Yes, I need to wake up first. How did you sleep?"

"Amazing. The sheets smell like us." Cate was red-faced.

"My beautiful Cate." Hunter kissed her mouth.

"Maybe I could convince you to stay?" Cate flirted.

"Just let me go check on this and we can spend the evening together."

"It's cold out. The windows are all frosted over. I'll make you some coffee to take with you. So, how are you going to approach them?" Cate asked as she poured water in the coffee pot.

"Well, I'm going to see how many there are, first. I will tell them they need to find somewhere else to go. The cabin isn't safe. It's falling apart." Hunter put his boots on.

"I could go with you," Cate offered.

"I won't be gone long. We could reheat the soup and have a drink by the fire when I get back."

"A woman's place is in the home?" Cate rang in, handing Hunter a cup of coffee.

"You said it, I didn't. Besides, I like you here." Hunter reassured. "We will have a peaceful evening when I get back. Let's leave early tomorrow to get back to Smokey. I miss him."

"You know that I come with Smokey, right? We're a package deal." Cate sassed.

"I'm going to hold you to that." Hunter beamed. He sauntered over to the gun case and retrieved his Father's rifle and ammunition.

Cate's eyes filled with concern. "Do you really need that?"

"It's just for protection. Don't worry, love."

The night air was sharp and invigorating. Hunter flipped his collar up to create a barrier against the bitter cold. The moon lit up the already beaten path. He didn't use his flashlight to alert them, hoping for the element of surprise to catch the kids in the act.

There was just enough snow to reveal the many animal hoof prints. Beady little round eyes peered out from the trees, focusing on Hunter's every move. The snowy bushes created an improvised shelter for the wild animals. Hunter always had a soft spot for wildlife. Their innocence and loyalty were a trait few humans shared.

As Hunter traveled deep into the forest a troubling memory invaded his brain.

"Lisa see those frogs there. Roll up your pant legs and grab me one I will show you a trick." Stan chewed on his half-lit cigarette butt.

"I don't want to Stan. Leave the frogs alone. You're just showing off for the neighbor girls." Lisa spat with anger.

"If I have to go into the creek and fetch a frog, you will pay for it later." Stan threatened.

Lisa waded into the water green moss stuck to her feet she imagined what aquatic creatures swam beneath the surface. She said a short prayer under her breath, sorry for the frog. And if there were monsters below the surface, she hoped they would devour Stan in one swoop! She closed her eyes and shoves her hand in the cold water grabbing the first slimy frog she could catch.

Stan ripped it from her hand. "Ladies, let's start fireworks a little early."

"No, Stan, please! I will let you have my favorite record! You can have my allowance! Please don't!" Lisa's voice trembled.

"This is what happens when you're weak and insignificant, Lisa. It's all about power. Now light it." Stan held the frog's mouth open and shoved a firecracker in.

"I don't have a lighter." Lisa tried to stall.

Stan stared. "Here, use my smoke."

Lisa stole the smoke out of his large hand and threw it in the creek. She ran away as fast as she could. A loud bang with girls shrieking and screaming indicated Stan had killed the frog. Lisa would have to deal with him later, but he couldn't force her to light the fuse.

There was the cabin, still dark. Hunter hid behind a tree to observe with his binoculars. Even though it was dark the moon radiated enough light to see shadows. After a while Hunter was getting cold and was thinking about leaving when he heard a branch crack and voices talking.

Two shadowy figures appeared, one tall and broad with a heavy backpack, and the other small and clumsy. Hunter decided to wait a few minutes and see what they were up to. After they went inside, he moved closer to the cabin and crouched down below the window.

"Help me get things set up! We don't have all night," a gruff voiced barked.

Hunter listened as the shadowy figures moved things around, dropping things — cans, boxes? — on the floor.

"We need to be careful. Are you listening? We will blow this place up if we're not careful. I can't afford to screw this up. Hold the flashlight still!" The same voice was yelling orders.

"I'm doing the best I can." A softer voice snapped back. "If you're worried about blowing the place up then stop yelling at me! I can't focus."

A woman. Hunter thought to himself.

"Bitch! Don't forget who you're talking to! Remember I can make you go away too!"

"Stan, you need to calm down! You need my help."

Hunter's blood ran cold, and the air stung his eyes. It can't be. Hunter mumbled to himself. The next couple minutes Hunter was in a state of disbelief. Get it together Hunter, you need to think!

"I'm in charge, Wendy. Steady your hands. This is the tricky part. We need to get this lab set up, make the goods, and head back. If you even think about skimming off the top, you will be swimming with the fishes!"

Brandi's face penetrated the walls of Hunter's brain. A sinking feeling churned in his gut. He had to get back to the cabin and alert the authorities. This situation moved past Hunter's own agenda with Stan. He would protect Cate and get justice for Brandi. He slowly moved back into the darkness for cover. Hunter needed to hurry.

CHAPTER 12

As he stumbled through the snow, Hunter's mind flew in a thousand directions. Stan never wanted to come up here when they were kids. Stan wasn't interested unless he could go down in the fields and get drunk. The cabin was something only Hunter shared with their father. Their other sister would stay with their mother, and as Stan become older, he was in and out of the juvenile system until he went to prison. Now he was back. This was Hunter's chance to make things right. Hunter ran inside the main cabin, slammed the door, and locked it.

"Is everything OK?" Cate wiped her hands on the dish towel.

"I need you to listen very carefully to me. Sit down." Hunter's hands were trembling as he found his way to the scotch on the old oak table.

"Hunter, what's going on?" Cate sat beside him.

"Stan is here in the cabin with a woman named Wendy. They're making some sort of lab to produce drugs! He is wanted for Brandi's murder. We need to call the police!"

"Are you sure it's him?" Cate shrieked.

"Positive!" Hunter reached for his phone. "It's dead! Let me use yours."

Cate didn't comprehend what Hunter was saying on the phone to the police. The shock was setting in and it paralyzed her. She managed to pull herself together when she realized the opportunity Hunter and she were presented with. Brandi's parents could have justice for the atrocities committed against their daughter. The same injustices Cate was subjected to as Edward, old scars. Below the surface there was still bleeding, seeping. Waiting for the perfect moment to reveal itself in its pure raw form to receive exoneration so the wound could heal from the inside out. Cate despised men who abused women in any way. Being a nurse, she was exposed to horrific encounters with domestic abuse, some deadly. Her own experience had almost crippled her. She felt guilty making this crisis about her feelings, but the rage filled her chest. Stan had caused enough damage.

He had to be stopped. He fell into the same category as the men she was subjected to in foster care.

Edward, come sit on my lap, I can show you how to drive. They fondled him; his manhood expanding in his summer shorts caused him disgust, a double betrayal. He became a plaything for every foster family. When they weren't feeling him up, they would use him as a punching bag, or dress him up as a girl and lock him outside for everyone to see. As long as they got their check, they kept Edward around to humiliate.

"Cate! Cate! The police are here! I'm going to go outside and talk to them." Hunter stated putting on his stocking cap. Hunter raised his hands up as he went outside to play it safe.

"Turn around and walk back toward my voice." An office barked orders at him.

"I'm not the one you're looking for!" Hunter shouted. "My brother is the one you want."

"What's your name?" The officer placed an artist sketch up to his face.

"Hunter! Stan and I do look alike, but we're different, trust me." Hunter didn't want to disclose the obvious reason. Police were not very friendly with Hunter's kind. So, he had to think fast. "Stan is taller than me. He also has a skull and crossbones tattoo on his right forearm."

"We will go down on foot. You go inside. We will be in touch." They gathered their gear and disappeared into the wood line.

Cate was thankful that Hunter went outside. She needed a few minutes to calm herself.

Hunter came in and locked the door again. "They are heading down to the cabin on foot. The police car will stay here. We're supposed to stay inside and wait." His face was etched with worry.

He took her hands to reassure her. "Don't worry, we will get through this. I'll talk to Robert. We need to board up the old cabins. No one else will use the cabins for illegal activity." Hunter held Cate close to his frame.

Both Hunter and Cate paced the floor looking out the window. Finally, a light bounced up and down through the trees, and four shadows emerged from the woods.

Each police officer directed their captives, Stan, and Wendy, with a jerk of the handcuffs gripping their wrists. As they walked closer Hunter saw his brother staring at the cabin. His body language was tight and aggressive.

"He knows it's me," Hunter said out loud.

"He knows what?" Cate went to the window as they put Stan in the car, she caught a glimpse of his face.

His face flickered like flash cards in her brain, familiar. And then Cate stopped dead in her tracks, knocking her over like a freight train.

"Hunter, it's him!" Cate stammered.

"Who?" Hunter walked past her avoiding eye contact.

"The man at the concert! It's him! He drugged me!"

"Are you sure? That night, you were really messed up." Hunter started pacing again.

"Yes, I was out of it. But you broke the window, and I came to. I saw you and I was yelling. He was yanking my hair to keep me in. I remember now." Cate crossed her arms deep in her own thoughts. "Wait." Cate turned around.

"You knew. You had to! Hunter, did you?"

Hunter took a deep breath and sat at the kitchen table. Cate's face was set in stone, her eyes stern and fiery with anger. Hunter knew he had messed up.

"Yes, I did know it was Stan," Hunter admitted.

Cate slammed her scotch glass hard on the table, torpedoing the ice cubes through the air. "How could you keep that from me? Were you trying to protect him by not going to the police?"

"Cate, how could you even think that?" Hunter replied incredulously. "I was trying to protect you!"

"Protect me from what? You? When were you going to tell me that you look almost identical?" Cate interrogated. "Now it makes sense. It's perfectly clear. Why wouldn't you have turned him in that night? Why, Hunter? Unless you two were in on it together?"

Hunter couldn't look at Cate. He was pissed at himself for not thinking this all the way through.

"Answer me now, Hunter!" Cate screamed.

"Please calm down," Hunter pleaded.

"Don't tell me to calm the fuck down! I'm not Susie who you can push around! I was assaulted, beaten, drugged and almost raped and you knew who it was? And it's a family member? You know deep down I was trying to figure out why you didn't want to go to the police. Now I know." Cate went into the bedroom and started throwing her clothes on the bed.

"We can't go anywhere. Besides, I drove up here." Hunter scoffed.

"Oh, you're going to keep me hostage now. You're just like Stan, aren't you? I don't even know who you are anymore!" Cate muttered through her tears, jamming her clothes into her overnight bag.

Hunter wrung his hands together. "Cate you must believe me. I was going to tell you. But first, I had to convince the police that I wasn't him when they saw me. Then I was going to tell you when we were waiting."

"You have known for a while now, Hunter. You had plenty of time." She wanted to scratch his eyes out. "Here I am letting my guard down, trusting you, falling in love! And you lie to me! Just like all the others!" Cate raged.

"What was that? I'm not like the others. I'm here!" Hunter slammed his fists on the table. "Just give me a moment to explain."

"I don't want to hear your bullshit, Hunter. Us, all of this. It's a farce. Maybe deep-down Lisa liked what her sick and twisted brother did to her all those years! You didn't go to the police then — why now! Maybe you're still protecting him!"

Cate sat back down, staring straight ahead with her arms folded. She didn't care that she was being cruel. Cate wanted him to experience her pain. She wanted to break his heart.

"How could you even think that?" Hunter exploded, picking up a chair and throwing it into the wall, covering the kitchen with debris and splinters of wood. "You think I'm like Stan, I can show you Stan."

The pressure from clenching his teeth felt like it would crack Hunter's jaw. He seized the scotch bottle and took a long hard drink.

Cate was a little afraid. She knew that she had pushed him too hard. But his lie shook her to the core.

"Are you done breaking furniture? I need you to tell me. Give me a reason not to walk out the front door, rescue my cat, and never talk to you again."

"Just like you did Michael?" Hunter poured another drink.

Cate's eyes went hollow and red, brimming with tears. "I'm leaving." She started toward the door.

Hunter stood in front keeping Cate from passing him. "Wait! It's freezing outside!"

"So? It's better than being in here with a liar!" Cate pounded on Hunter's bear like chest until she collapsed from exhaustion.

"I hate you! How could you Hunter? I love you!" Cate groaned through her sobs.

Hunter sat her on the couch and knelt to talk softly to her.

"Listen. I'm telling you the truth. When I showed up at the concert, I was looking for Stan. Finally, I had mustered up enough courage to pursue him. The concert was a way to run into him. Stan never misses a big event to help camouflage selling drugs and finding girls to pimp out. I saw you there, then he came up with a beer for you. So, I followed you and well, you know the rest." Hunter was sweaty and tired. "You were so reckless! Why were you having drinks with some strange man at a concert? Did you want to sleep with him?" Hunter demanded.

"Why didn't you tell me? You could have told me once I was safe. You kept it from me on purpose!" Cate growled.

"No! you're not putting this on me. I was trying to protect you and you were out looking for a fuck!" Hunter sent his drinking glass sailing through the air where it exploded against the wall sending pieces of jagged glass back towards them.

"Who are you trying to protect me from? You?" Cate yelled.

Hunter shoved the refrigerator door closed after snatching a beer.

"You need to calm the fuck down, Hunter. I'm not going to put up with your temper." Cate added. "So, what, I went out to listen to some music and have a drink." Cate didn't want to mention that she was hoping to run into him. This was not the right moment to explain why she had a drink with his carbon copy.

"Fine! If you really need to know I didn't want you to connect his face with mine. Especially when we make love. I don't want you to see him. I want you to see me. That's the truth." She had to hear him. "And Cate, you haven't been exactly honest with me." Hunter exclaimed, taking a big gulp of beer.

"What do you mean?" Cate's foot started to shake.

Hunter went into the bedroom and came out with his pill bottle slamming it down on the table. "This!" Hunter pointed at the bottle. "Cate, I count my pills so I can keep track of them. You're stealing them from me I'm short! And I also found a pill under my bed at the house. I'm glad that I did. Smokey could have eaten it."

Cate swallowed hard before she spoke. "My headaches are coming back so I've been taking a few at night."

"You're an addict. So, you think it's perfectly OK to steal my pills that I need from my surgery." Hunter stormed. "You're lying. I can see it in your face. How many chances do you think you will get? You could go to jail this time, Cate. They might not let you go to rehab again."

"I don't need to explain myself." Cate snarled. "And you haven't been taking any of those pills for months." Cate dismissed him with a flick of her manicured hand.

"That's not the fucking point! I'm going out to get some firewood." Hunter banged the door hard. He reached in his coat pocket and pulled out a cigarette. I need to get it together.

Hunter stood out in the cold and tugged hard on his smoke, trying to figure out what happened in there. As he looked out into the darkness, he knew one thing for sure. I love her. He didn't want to, because right now he was angry. But the guilt began to slowly chip away at him. She was right. He should have told her, but he was scared. Afraid to face the truth with Stan. It was easy to say he was trying to protect Cate. But facing Stan terrified him.

Inside, Cate drifted into the bedroom and sagged on the bed. She knew how difficult she was. What does it matter? He knows the truth now. He will leave; they all do. Cate unscrewed his bottle and greedily took two more pills. Hunter was lying. Maybe she was protecting her, but he was also protecting himself. She needed him to say that. Then maybe she could finally tell him her ugly truth and not be crippled when he left.

Hunter gathered some firewood and headed back. The wind was sharp and unforgiving. He went back inside and fed the fire. Cate was asleep in the bedroom. He fetched a blanket and covered her up and located a blanket, settling on the couch for the night. Maybe tomorrow would be better.

The next morning the birds woke Hunter up. Everything was a little fuzzy. They were heading back today. Smokey would be missing them, and Cate needed to go back to work tomorrow. The cabin was a mess. Broken glass, wood splinters, and the smell of liquor permeated the room like the remnants of a bar room brawl.

Coffee. Hunter took a sleepy step towards the kitchen. "Dammit!" A large shard of glass bulged out the side of his foot. He jumped on one foot back to the couch leaving blood drops behind him. "Cate, I cut myself!"

Cate poked her head around the door and scoffed. "For such a big man you sound like a little girl." She grabbed a towel and some tweezers and pushed him back onto the couch. "Sit still."

"Little girl! Not funny" Hunter muttered as she pulled at the glass. "Shit! Cate go a little easy, will you?"

"You will be all right; besides, I'm still pissed at you. It's in there deep. Got it!" Cate held the tweezers up so Hunter could see. Do you have anything to clean it out? Besides hot water and soap?" Cate asked.

"I'm not sure." Hunter rubbed his face trying to get the sleep out of his eyes. "We need a first aid kit. I think there is something in the kitchen drawer."

"I found the kit. We can use a little bit of this, too." Cate had the bottle of scotch in her other hand.

"I would rather drink it." Hunter mentioned with a condescending tone. "Fuck! That really hurts."

"It can't be more than your bottom surgery!" Cate spoke with sarcasm. "You really don't have a very high pain tolerance, Hunter." Cate squeezed the gauze tightly.

"Fuck, Cate, be a little gentle!" Hunter jerked his foot away.

"Your little cut fails in comparison to what I'm subjected to day in and day out."

"Sorry. How much do I owe you, doc?" Hunter pulled back, a little tentatively. It had been a terrible fight. Could she forgive?

"Nothing. But let's go. I need to get back home soon." Cate wanted to be alone. The sooner she made it home the better.

Hunter watched her put away the kit and start the coffee. He wanted to tell her how much she meant to him, to remind her he was falling in love. But he might have already scared her away.

He limped into the kitchen, careful to avoid the shattered glass. "I'm so sorry for not telling you about Stan. I always had your best interests at heart. My temper gets the best of me, I know, and I'm still working on that. I'm passionate. What can I say?" Hunter walked on his heel over to the kitchen to retrieve the broom and dustpan.

Cate bit her lip to try and contain her tears. She still felt violated and angry. "I'm sorry too." Cate looked directly at Hunter. "I'm sorry that you found it necessary to lie to me. But I question your motives. We were special. Now we're tainted." Cate's voice cracked. She went to the bedroom and continued packing.

Hunter limped to the bedroom, his head pounding.

He wrapped his arms around her nestling in her hair which still smelled of wildflowers.

"Hunter, don't." Cate folded her last shirt and picked up her suitcase. "If you had my best interests at heart, you would have told me. You were protecting yourself, not me. Can we go? I need to get back. Will you be able to drive with your foot?"

"I'm fine!" Hunter shot back. The light on his phone displayed a missed call.

"I have a voicemail. The police want me to come down to the station tomorrow to give a statement." Hunter was relieved that Stan was in custody. A faint smile spread across his lips. He is going down this time.

The drive home should have been soothing and beautiful. The mountains, blue streams, and majestic wildlife colored the landscape all around them. But they rode in silence, hoping to clear their heads, with aching hearts.

Cate was tired of being angry. She wanted to break the tension and caught a glimpsc of thc powerful painting in the backseat.

"Where do you think you will hang your uncle's painting?"

"Well, I was thinking maybe my office. It's a very commanding picture. It would inspire me."

"Speaking of your writing, I would still love to read some. How can you be a writer and so private about who reads it?"

"I'm superstitious. I like to wait till I'm finished," Hunter lied.

"Is there something that you don't want me to, see?" Cate insisted. "Do you have more secrets?" Cate looked out the window.

"Of course not. I'm.... just not ready yet." Hunter stumbled.

"Hunter." Cate said softly. "I have been lied to my whole life. My teachers told Edward he could be anything he wanted. Being told he could act "normal" so some family will adopt him. I knew I wanted to become a woman. I had to make that happen. It wasn't like wishing on a falling star. Finally, by the time I fostered out of the system, I had figured it out. People lie to protect themselves. That's all. Lies. No one adopted me and I could never be normal. So, I learned to lie too, protecting myself from Gwen, Michael, my job, even myself. No, I haven't stopped taking pills and yes, I steal them from work and patients who die. I'm not proud of it. There it is. Now you can leave me for real." Cate buried her head while her tears welled up and rolled down her cheeks. "And yes, I stole your medication. But you lied too."

Hunter didn't know what to say so he just listened, waiting. But she didn't say anything else.

They arrived at Cate's just before dusk. "Here, let me help you." Hunter carried her bag and watched her open the door.

"I'll bring it in. You just go home." Cate barked at him.

"I will check upstairs." Hunter tried not to notice the pile of clothes and garbage overflowing in the kitchen. It reaffirmed Cate's story about struggling. But he wasn't going to give up on her. He was going to prove to her that he was staying.

"I can stay and help you clean up the place." Hunter offered.

"That's OK. Smokey is waiting and you need to get ready to go to the police station. I will pick him up tomorrow. I want a bath and I'm going to bed early. Let me know what happens after you give your statement."

"Can we talk about this?"

"Hunter, I need some time. You hurt me."

"I don't want you to take Smokey. Don't give up on us, Cate." Hunter sighed.

"He's coming home with me tomorrow. I just need time."

Cate slowly closed the door. Emptiness tugged hard in Hunter's chest. All his instincts told him they were done. He just wanted to get back home. Smokey would have missed him, and they didn't have much more time together.

Pulling up into the driveway he saw a fluffy body peering out from the windowsill. When he heard the key in the lock, Smokey scratched at the door and howled.

"Are you hungry, boy? You want some food?"

Hunter made himself a sandwich and popped open a can of food for Smokey. He decided to try and work for a while to keep his mind off tomorrow. Smokey lay by his feet and kept them warm.

CHAPTER 13

After a restless night, Cate was running late and frazzled. She hit snooze on her alarm and fell asleep again, and then didn't have her uniform ready for work. She tried to ignore the pungent smell of garbage as she gulped down cold coffee, made toast for the road. She found her cleanest uniform on and shook it out. It would do.

She reached in her overnight bag from the weekend to grab her compact and found her pill bottle instead. Her insides began to twist, she started to sweat, and she held the bottle in a tight grip.

No, I'm not doing this. I'm quitting for Hunter and me.

Cate headed out the door in a hurry. Everything that could go wrong had gone wrong. But in that moment, for the first time in a long time she didn't panic. She hadn't used. Maybe I can beat this.

Smokey was hungry and wanted attention. He bumped Hunter's face hard and tapped his furry pads on his face, gently licking his beard.

"Good morning, boy." Hunter closed his eyes a few more minutes while Smokey purred on his chest. It was a beautiful morning. The only person missing was Cate. Hunter fed Smokey and jumped in the shower while the coffee perked. Today he would make his statement at the police station. For once, all he felt was clarity —the rage had eased in his limbs and chest. There was no need for vengeance; Stan had set himself up, finally. Hunter was ready to let go. But he would get satisfaction. He could take Stan out quietly and without warning. He was going to ambush his brother.

Hunter despised going downtown. The dilapidated buildings and graffiti were a warning to any outsider. Junkies on every street corner, their eyes blank or anguished, painted a picture of a once promising life in a dying city. Working girls bartered their bodies for drugs or food for a child left at home by themselves. Lost people. Maybe they were doomed from day one.

He remembered Wendy, and how close Lisa had been to that life. What Stan had done to Lisa was almost insignificant now. The statement Hunter was about to give was for Cate, and Wendy, Brandi, all the other young girls whose futures Stan stole. Revenge had evolved into something much bigger.

"Can I help you?" A petite, attractive female officer looked up from her paperwork.

"Yes, I'm here to speak to Officer Jones about making a statement."

"OK, let me round him up. There is some fresh coffee made. Help yourself."

The young police officer was curious. Hunter saw her eyes darting up and down his body. It took him a moment to realize she was flirting with him. He stood straighter and gave her an amused look. It was good to be a man.

The coffee was strong, so Hunter added some cream and sugar for courage. He needed all the energy he could muster today. It might be a long one.

The door squeaked open and a robust detective with a receding hairline and caterpillar mustache emerged.

"Hunter, thank you for coming. My office is this way."

As they walked down the hallway, Hunter's senses were on high alert. He knew that Stan was in a holding cell, and he wanted to be prepared for any confrontation.

"Have a seat. We need to confirm some information about Stan and have you ID him as the man you saw in the cabin. First, how are you related to Stan?"

"I'm his younger brother." Hunter replied without hesitation.

The officer set his pen down and sat back in his chair. "That's funny. He said that he has two sisters he hasn't spoken to for years. The only thing that convinces me that you're related is the police report and the family resemblance. Do you have a driver's license?"

Hunter dug inside his faded motorcycle wallet and tossed it on the table. He was irritated but tried to remain focused. This was just a distraction.

Detective Jones studied the picture and the information. When he was satisfied, he tossed it back.

"I tell you what. I'm quite sure I understand what's going on here. And I'm not interested in your past. That's your business, Hunter. Let's focus on your brother. Now, tell me about him, and how you came to know Brandi. Include anything you know about Stan's plan to make methamphetamines on your property."

Hunter spent the next couple hours explaining his encounter with Brandi, from their flirtation to her O.D. When he had nothing to add about Stan's drug business, the detective looked dubious. Hunter could sense by the incessant pen tapping across the desk that the cop wasn't happy with the information he was providing. He started to worry that he wouldn't be able to confront Stan after all and might even get in trouble for all his effort.

"So, I'm supposed to believe you didn't have sex with her? You were the last person to see her, according to the bartender."

"Look, detective, I was told to come down and give a statement. Now you know what I know. I didn't realize that I was going to be interrogated." The corners of his mouth tightened along with his fists.

"I'm just doing my job. Can't blame me for that, right? We have a dead young woman whose family is asking me questions. We found DNA on the victim and are waiting on results which take some time. Stan will be kept here until we can move forward."

"Detective, I want to talk to him." Hunter spoke sharply.

"We can't do that. It's too much of a risk. He'll just shut down even more. After all, he hasn't even acknowledged you, as his brother." The detective gave Hunter a long look. Hunter didn't flinch, and moved in.

"What if I can get him to talk? You will be listening, of course." Hunter suggested. Hunter could see the wheels turning in the detective's head. Hunter had to see Stan. "Trust me, he will have plenty to say to me. There's a good reason he hasn't mentioned me. I know him better than anyone. Maybe I get a confession and then with the DNA against him – and I'm sure it's his.... Brandi's murder fits his pattern, believe me. It could be a slam dunk."

"Wait here. I will be back." The detective disappeared into the hallway.

Hunter's thoughts circled like a fish in a fishbowl. It's going to happen. You must believe it. He started imagining facing Stan down.

Violent images exploded in his memory. Part of him wanted to smash Stan's face in. Another part wanted to torture him and make him squeal in pain. But all of him wanted Stan to be vulnerable and afraid, uncertain of his future. When he's convicted and sent to prison for life the tables will have finally turned on him. I'll be the alpha male then. There is always someone bigger and tougher than you, Stan. Karma delivers her verdict.

Hunter could hear footsteps coming closer and the detective stuck his head back into the office. "OK, I have some officers setting some equipment up in the other room so we can record your conversation. This wire you can wear under your shirt. I'll help you set it up. Take it off here — we need the tape to stick."

Hunter delayed for a moment. He knew there would be questions about his scars, and he really didn't want to explain. But he took his shirt off and hoped for the best. To his surprise, the Detective taped the wire on with no questions. Hunter was relieved.

"Stan will be handcuffed, and a police officer will be right outside that door. We're trying to make it look as if we are not interested in your conversation. Good luck."

The room felt small, and the walls were slowly closing in. Perspiration surfaced down his back and chest causing his clothes to stick to his skin. I hope the wire will stay in place. Hunter thought to himself.

As he walked down the hall with the detective, he heard every noise. Keys jingling, echoing steps, pieces of conversations. Each step brought him closer to Stan. This was it. All the pain and rage and trauma focused into one goal: get his brother to confess. Break him. The door opened and there was Stan, disheveled and hateful. He looked up, unblinking.

"Who the fuck are you?" Stan growled.

"My name is Hunter."

"Is that supposed to mean something to me? I'm not going to talk to you, either, whoever you are."

"You will eventually." Hunter smiled a little.

The heat and rage burning from Stan's icy cold eyes was familiar. He needed to maintain his control.

"Do you know a girl named Brandi?"

Stan scoffed at the question, clearly irritated "I know a lot of girls."

"Well, she sure knew you."

"Is there a point to this, pretty boy? Isn't it time for my lunch?" Stan hissed.

"Do you have a sister named Lisa?" Hunter asked, feeling calm spread through his whole body.

Stan's eyes widened at the corners and his jaw began twitching. Hunter clearly hit a nerve. Stan was his prey now. He shifted in his chair and the handcuffs rattled a little.

There was a pause, and then Stan seemed to recover. "Who wants to know?" Stan spat and turned away.

"Brandi, Lisa and I hung out for a while." Hunter leaned back. "We would drink a few beers, play pool. We met in the local bar."

Hunter had forgotten how easy it was to read Stan's face. How his jaw would tighten when he was avoiding an issue, or when he wasn't getting what he wanted. How the veins on his forehead would bulge from stress that could only be released in violence or sex.

Stan tilted forward. "Why do I give a shit?"

"Brandi talked about you a lot. How you found her on the street. Took her in, showered her with gifts, a place to stay, all the drugs she wanted. But you had strings, didn't you? Get her hooked-on drugs, have her on the streets hooking to pay you back. She finally knew you had exploited her. She lost everything. She fought back, didn't she?" Hunter bent forward to meet Stan's eyes.

Stan flashed a wicked smile and Hunter caught a glimpse of his silver tooth. "Sounds like I treated her well, considering, if I knew her at all. From the sound of it, she was an addict and I'm sure she slept with men to get her fix. They do that. Anyway, I told you I know a lot of girls. If I knew her, she wouldn't stand out. Anyway, how does this concern you? Are you working for the pigs?" Stan's dirty fingers tapped on the table.

"Brandi was my friend. I want to find out what happened to her. I think you know. Because Lisa talked about all the things you did to her, too. All those nights you would come into her room and do unspeakable things to her. Getting her high. Drugging her friends. Pimping your own sister out. Your sister. Remember?" Hunter kept pushing.

With a crash, the chair flew backwards as Stan stood up. His eyes were glazed over like a crazed animal. "I don't know who the fuck you think you are. But I will crush your skull!"

"You can't hurt me! You will never touch me again, you fucking monster! All those years you violated me. Coming in my room stinking up the place with booze and cigarettes. I didn't even know then what it was, what you took, but you stole my innocence. It wasn't enough. You wanted my life. Your sense of entitlement is nauseating. But you were always pitiful. Poor Stan! You had it so hard, right?" Hunter's voice deepened into a sound that mirrored Stan's. "Dad loved you more, Lisa! No one visited me in prison!"

Hunter narrowed his eyes. "Why do you think our sister moved away? To escape you! Your depravity! And to keep her children away from you! No one wanted to be near you, Stan. You're toxic."

All the color drained from Stan's face. His knees buckled and he fumbled to find the chair to sit down in. His ice blue eyes darted up and down Hunter's face.

"Lisa? It can't be." Stan shook his head back and forth in disbelief.

"Now I have your attention." Hunter said simply and sat back again.

"Wow! You look like me — I always knew you were a freak. I guess that means you don't hate me. You must admire me. I bet you're just like me now. You need to see a shrink, Lisa."

Hunter bit back a curse and let Stan stew.

Stan studied him for a long minute, his jaw tight. "Wait a minute, I recognize — that blonde bitch — you saved her. I guess you wanted her all for yourself. Tell me something, how can you please a babe like her without a dick? Because you'll never have a dick like mine, Lisa. You freak!" Stan sneered, confident again. "By the way, you owe me a new window."

Hunter was quiet for a minute. The officers were watching. Stan liked to talk. Try to keep him bragging. "Maybe. Maybe not. I'm curious, Stan. The river where they found Brandi's body — have you been there before?"

"I want an attorney. I don't have to talk to anyone, especially you. Fuck you! Officer, I'm ready to go!"

Stan smiled wide showing his jagged teeth. Hunter knew Stan thought he won but he hadn't. He couldn't. "Don't you remember? I'll help you out. The river where you dumped Brandi's body is where you took me to rape me. Where you raped Wendy, too, I bet." Hunter's eyes turned dark and pierced right through Stan's protective armor.

"Guard, I want to go now!" Stan screamed. "You're a fucking freak! You deserve everything I gave you and more. I was trying to help you become a real woman but instead you turned yourself into some side show attraction. No wonder Sara didn't want anything to do with you!"

Hunter was ready to go in for the kill. "You were the freak, Stan. I was always Dad's favorite, wasn't I? He always took me to go to cabin with him. You embarrassed him, Stan. What you are disgusted him. So, he left me the cabins after he died. Because you were dead to him. That's my land, not yours. You have no right to it."

"Fuck you, Lisa!" Stan's mouth hung open in pure astonishment as he said her name. Hunter relished Stan's confusion with his wheels turning trying to put the pieces of the puzzle together. "If Dad was alive, you would be the shame of the family. They should have sent you away to fix your crazy mind!" Stan yelled.

Hunter pounced forward, placing his large fists on the table, and looked straight at Stan. "Dad loved me. He knew who I am. Me. Hunter. And I'm more man than you will ever be! All you have to look forward to is being someone's bitch in prison. I hope you're raped every day and beaten to a pulp. I hope you stay alive in there a long time! Karma, Stan. It's coming for you. Because of what you did to me. To all those other women. To Brandi."

Stan's crazed eyes exploded with fury. The table went flying over and the guard rushed in to subdue Stan. "I should have killed you and put you in the river, then you would have been there to keep Brandi company when I finished her off. Fish food, both of you! No one would miss you, you freak, and no one misses that bitch. She stole from me, then she laughed at me. No one does that!" Stan screamed.

Hunter smiled with relief. He knew that Stan had sealed his own coffin. All Lisa's pain and resentment were vindicated. Hunter's self-inflicted prison bars dissolved.

He could begin to live his life as Hunter. There was still a long way for him to go, but the slate was clean, and he held the chalk now. "Good-bye, Stan. I know you'll think of me often. But I will not waste another minute thinking of you. Don't bother to write!" Hunter chuckled.

Officers dragged Stan out the door. The detective came in with a towel and a cup of coffee.

"Cream and sugar, right? Here is a towel to wipe the sweat off. Careful, the tape sometimes pulls your hair."

Hunter took his shirt off and wiped his scarred chest and face. The officer bundled up the wire and shook his hand.

"Good job, Hunter. We should have enough to stick. I have a feeling this will go to trial, though. Stan won't give in. Don't worry — he isn't going anywhere. Thank you for your help."

Hunter wanted to go home and shower and sleep. He was mentally and physically exhausted. The hot coffee warmed him. He hadn't realized how tired and cold he felt, as if he'd had a fever and it had finally broken. He would call Cate right away and tell her the good news. She would forgive him, he knew, when she found out. From now on, everything would be right in his world.

Over the next few months Hunter and Cate's relationship flourished. They spent weekends together, cuddling and watching movies with Smokey by their side.

Hunter's book was almost finished. He finally was free to share the viciousness and cruelty he experienced as a child with her. After confronting Stan, he was able to love Lisa and now, as Hunter. Something beautiful emerged from that horrible time.

Hunter had been just too immersed in his pain to notice how much love he'd always had. He was luckier than Cate. Robert and his father may not have always agreed or understood his choices, but they allowed him room to explore and navigate his own life. Even Hunter's mother was tolerant of his two-spirit nature. He grew more and more grateful, gradually growing into a blissful being of hope.

Finally, Hunter decided to ask Cate to move in. Smokey was at his place all the time and he had fallen hard for her. She was doing great at work. It was the logical next step.

"Hey Smokey, your mom is on her way. Should we tell her how much you miss her when she's not here?" Hunter patted Smokey gently and scratched under his chin.

Smokey darted off his lap and popped his head in between the curtains. Hunter was thrilled to hear Cate's car in the driveway.

Hunter went out to help Cate with her bags.

"I can carry one little bag, silly." Cate's eyes sparkled.

"Well, what if I'm trying to impress you?" Hunter teased back. "Preparing a proper seduction…."

"That could be arranged." Cate playfully touched Hunter's defined biceps.

After dinner, Hunter and Cate cuddled in the living room.

"So, I talked to the detective today about Stan. They offered him a plea deal, but he won't accept it. He will go to trial. It's so like him to deny everything even when they have DNA and a confession." Hunter ranted.

"The confession he gave you wasn't good enough to convict him?" Cate added.

"Stan's attorney says it was coerced out of him. But that won't stick. He should take the plea deal. He will get life for sure now." Hunter paused. "I finished my book. I want you to read it." Hunter handed it to her.

Cate was astonished. "Are… you sure?" She paused.

"I'm sorry that I wasn't ready before now. I had to finish it."

"Well, if you feel up to it. I would love to hear some of your story first. From you. It will make the book even better…." Cate veered her body closer to him.

"I don't know where to start." Hunter confessed.

"Any place you feel comfortable." Cate said encouraging him.

"Well, I was in love only once. Or I thought I was. The boys made it a joke, though, my brother and his friends. One on one they always liked me. We would drink beer and smoke weed listen to music. So, I thought they were trying to be my friends.

"Friends! After I was drunk and high, they would profess their undying love to me and how much they admired my athletic ability, just to get over. Some of the boys were smart enough not to call me beautiful — I didn't respond well to being treated like a girl. I was fine with kissing because I could imagine me kissing my girl crush — Sara. After a while, all their begging and pleading would wear on me so I would give in. Intercourse was off the table – you know, I didn't want to be femininized. But and I hope this makes sense, with oral sex I got my power back. I could decide how long it would last and I would float away out of my body.

"Of course, everyone said how easy I was. Until one day I had enough and stopped. I was in love – or I thought I was — with Sara. Never even touched her except in my mind a thousand times. I wanted to save myself for her. But — she didn't feel the same. My first broken heart."

"Hunter, I wish you would tell me about Stan." Cate couldn't help pushing. She wanted to know everything. "Did he… do things to you too?"

A tear fell down Hunter's face as he nodded. "How long have you known?" Hunter asked.

"I have always known."

Cate noticed Hunter's face was flushed and blotchy. This was hard for him, and Cate knew it. "I'm sorry that those boys took advantage of you and I'm sorry they didn't appreciate your beauty as a man. I'm sorry that Stan — I'm so sorry. But I see you. I see you completely." Cate kissed Hunter's neck.

A deep longing surged through his body and his senses were heightened. He took his shirt off as Cate kissed his chest and touched his thick lips with her fingers. The passion was so intense and electric that they had to have each other right there. Cate pushed Hunter back onto the carpet their hands were fumbling with buttons and zippers.

Cate moved Hunter inside of her with an animalistic desire. Hunter ran his hands all over Cate's body kissing her deep and letting her take him deeper inside her. Hunter's toes were beginning to curl as Cate's moved faster. Then she let out a deep moan and collapsed on his chest, overwhelmed by Hunter's rugged smell. He was right behind her, bucking and holding her hips still with his hands until he finished.

Hunter lay there, still inside her and not wanting to let go. They fell asleep holding each other for a few hours.

Hunter woke up to Cate sleeping next to him on the floor. He pulled a blanket from off couch and covered them up. He watched her sleep taking in her beauty. This beautiful creature has come into his life, and he wasn't going to let anything take her away.

"Hey gorgeous, my back is killing me! I'm not twenty-one anymore. I'm ready to go to bed."

Cate rubbed her eyes and walked toward the bedroom half asleep. Hunter fed Smokey and left the door open so the cat could join them later. The bed was warm and inviting.

"Cate." Hunter spoke quietly. "I've been thinking. I want us to be exclusive. You don't need to drive across town anymore. Smokey is here with me." Hunter reached over to nightstand and pulled out a house key and gave it to Cate. "Will you move in with me?"

Cate paused. "Hunter... I don't know. Just because we have great sex doesn't mean we should live together." She got out of bed and started to get dressed.

"So, that's it? This is as far you're willing to go with us. We have been dating almost a year. I mean I'm forty-two Cate. Are we doing this or not?" Hunter hiked his jeans up, almost falling over.

"Things are going well at work. I'm finally OK not using. I mean, my house is clean, what does that tell you? I mean, I would have to sell my house or find a renter. I don't know…" Cate trailed off.

"I know you're doing great! I'm proud of you. Living here won't change that. Cate, I can't just accept that answer! I'm in love with you and I want to be with you all the time." Hunter directed Cate around. "Wake up and let me love you."

But Cate dropped her eyes, so Hunter went out to the living room. He was starting to get mad, and he had to stay calm.

He cuddled up to Smokey on the couch. "I love you, too Smokey. I hope your mom knows that." By the front door, an envelope caught Hunter's eye.

"What's this?" Hunter said out loud.

> *Hunter, I hope things are going well for you and your writing is coming along with great success! I heard about Stan, and I must say it doesn't surprise me. He needs to sit in a cell and rot. Anyway, I've been thinking. Maybe we could go out to dinner or have a drink and catch up. The last time we saw each other wasn't under the best circumstance.*
> *Susie.*

"What are you reading?" Cate asked. She was dressed now, composed.

"Just a letter." Hunter stated cautiously.

"From?"

"Susie." Hunter said over his shoulder as he placed the letter back into the envelope.

"Why is she writing you? I didn't know you two were still talking." Cate looked straight at the floor.

"We have not had any contact since you and I started hanging out." Hunter knew not to keep anything from Cate.

"What does the letter say?" Cate bit her lip nervously.

"Here." Hunter passed the letter to her.

"It's addressed to you. I just want to know what this woman has to say." Cate frantically adjusted her hair in the living room mirror.

Hunter let out a big sigh. "She wants to have dinner and talk."

Cate stopped quickly. "Well, you know what that means."

"No... I don't." Hunter responded.

"Hunter please, it's obvious that she wants to get back together with you." Cate plopped onto the couch. Cate's jealousy always devoured her in one bite, leaving her uncertain and scared just like that night at the cabin.

"You need to choose Susie or me! Are you pretending you don't know what's going on because you want her back? Is it because she is a cis woman? Do you find her more attractive than me?" Cate's voice splintered off.

"Woah, wait a minute." Hunter raised his hands to declare truce. "First, I was going to show you the letter. Second, I wasn't going to respond to her. Cate I'm in love with you. I just asked you to move in with me!"

"But I only see you on the weekends. You could do anything you want during the week."

"Then move in, so you can keep an eye on me." Hunter dimpled flirtatiously.

"Hunter, I told you how I feel about that." Cate muttered as she escaped to the kitchen. She poured a glass of water and kept her back to him.

"You know what, Cate, you need to decide. This is not about Susie. Do you see a future with us or not? We're not fucking sixteen!" Hunter crossed his forearms flexing his muscles.

"OK, what if I did move in and this Susie woman comes back into the picture? I can't deal with that. I will not play second fiddle to another woman!"

"Don't I have any say about this? How do you go from me finding a letter that I didn't know anything about to a full-on relationship with Susie?" Hunter changed the clouded water in Smokey's bowl. The cat was his only friend and ally now.

"Hunter, you have a memory problem. Not too long ago you lied to me about Stan — and that lie nearly destroyed us!"

"I thought we were past that. I admitted that I was wrong, and you forgave me. You can't keep throwing it up in my face! Fuck!" Hunter reached for his cigarettes, but the pack was empty.

"Every time I fall in love, they pull the wool over my eyes. I won't let you do that again!"

"You're being irrational Cate. I want to be with you, not Susie." Hunter pulled on his shirt and shoes.

"Oh, so now I'm being irrational!" Cate raised her voice. "Where are you going?"

"To get some cigarettes!" Hunter growled.

"You have to stop smoking, Hunter!" Cate shouted.

Cate heard him slam the door. Her curiosity got the better of her and she went out to the living room to search for the letter. Then she noticed a piece of paper under Smokey's front paw.

"Thank you, Smokey." Cate petted his soft and fluffy fur. The letter confirmed her suspicions – Susie wanted him back. How could she compete?

"I don't know who this woman thinks she is, Smokey, but she isn't getting my man!" Cate hissed as she placed the letter back in the envelope. "Susie left Hunter when he needed her the most. How dare she think she can have him back? Not going to happen!"

Cate undressed and hopped in the shower. When Hunter got back, she would be perfect.

CHAPTER 14

Hunter parked in the driveway and smoked. He had to blow off some steam. Part of him was curious about why Susie felt the need to contact him. Part of him was disgusted. *You can't do this Susie. Walking out and thinking you can waltz back in! You chose to leave; I wasn't what you wanted. I love Cate! That's all I need to know now.*

He would tell Cate that he would call Susie and tell her he is in a relationship and going on a dinner date is not a good idea. He didn't want Cate to be uncomfortable. When he got back, Cate was sound asleep. He slept on the couch.

The next morning Hunter was up early to start an outline for a new story. Cate was still sleeping, and Smokey was in his assigned seat with his tail tucked around Hunter's feet.

Hunter was thankful the weather was starting to warm up. Soon he would go up to the cabin again. He loved to walk outside in his father's garden barefoot. The energy from the soil connected him to something deeper, almost primitive.

He and Robert would board up the unused cabins, and planting season was just around the corner, his favorite time of the year. Hunter had wanted to surprise Cate with the trip but after last night he didn't know how she would react. He didn't understand why she was still so upset. She hadn't waited up for him after he came back from the convenience store.

He decided he would try and quit smoking again after this pack was gone. He understood why Cate despised smoking. Her father had died from lung cancer. Gwen smoked. And in the medical field she had witnessed so many complications from smoking. If it made her happy…

A rapid knock at the front door sent Smokey darting to the kitchen. Hunter checked his watch. He wasn't expecting anyone. He went to the door and opened it.

"Hi Hunter, sorry to bother you. It looks like you have company." Susie pointed to Cate's car.

"As a matter of fact, I do. What can I help you with?"

"Did you get my letter?" Susie asked.

"Yes." Hunter was waiting for Cate to storm out of the bedroom at any moment.

"Can I come in?" Susie inquired.

"Yes, let her in Hunter." Cate's voice caught him off guard. She stood in his bedroom door, wearing her best clothes, fully made up. She was ready for war.

Hunter saw the disappointment in Susie's eyes. What does she expect? Hunter thought to himself. That he could still care after everything she had done?

Hunter knew Cate would be jealous. As Susie sat down Hunter put his arm around Cate's shoulder. "Susie, this is Cate. We're seeing each other."

"Nice to meet you." Susie spoke without emotion.

Cate's skin was burning hot, and she was finding it difficult to swallow. Susie's long black hair sparkled like diamonds in ink. Her white skin was flawless. Her eyes danced as she looked around the home she and Hunter had once shared. Then Cate smiled to herself when she remembered that whatever was left of Susie in the house was in a box in the closet. Cate had replaced the old interior decorations with her own. Still, she was having trouble looking at Susie. She looked like a model.

"I'm sorry." Susie blurted out. "I shouldn't have stopped by unannounced. I was in the neighborhood and thought I would drop in." Susie turned toward Hunter, shutting Cate out. "The newspaper's going crazy over Stan's case. They've moved it out of town even, with all the publicity. Personally, I wish the prosecution would weigh his ankles down with cement and throw him in the river and give that poor girl's family front row seats."

"Did you know Stan?" Cate interrupted.

"She met him a couple times." Hunter said tersely.

"I was asking Susie." Cate scolded.

Susie looked over at Hunter, as if she was asking for his permission to keep talking, which enraged Cate. She felt like Edward in drag, banging on the front door afraid the neighbors might see him. Begging his foster sisters to stop laughing, stop teasing. Let me in!

In the face of Hunter's silence, Susie explained. "Lis — Hunter's family had some type of reunion. As you can imagine we were the gossip of the town. I was relieved to see Hunter's cousin Robert — he was always very accepting and so was Hunter's father. Well, we made our rounds and had some barbecue when this old beater without a muffler pulls up. Stan and some woman practically fall out of the car, beer cans fly out onto the pavement."

"Susie, I think we get the picture. It was just Stan being his normal asshole self. A bad scene, Cate." Hunter stood up.

"I want to hear the story, Hunter. Go on, Susie, please." Cate sat down and bent forward.

"Well, they both came staggering up, drunk and hanging all over each other. Hunter didn't want to deal with Stan. The sight of him made Hunter sick, as you can imagine. So, he disappeared, talking to other people."

Hunter made a disgusted gesture. "Stan came up and sat down next to Susie and was flirting with her. He made such a huge scene when she rejected him that Robert asked him to leave.".

"I'm sure Stan didn't go quietly," Cate sniffed.

"No, he punched Robert and broke his nose." Susie giggled, and was distracted by Smokey, who bumped her leg. "Oh, Look at you!" Susie picked up Smokey and rubbed her face on his. "You're gorgeous!"

Cate wanted to hate her. She knew Susie wanted to snatch Hunter away.

"Hunter, your uncle's painting– it's beautiful!" Susie walked over and admired it.

The top two buttons on her sheer blouse were open and Cate knew it wasn't by accident. Cate adjusted her carefully chosen dress, disappointment branded across her face. Everything about Susie is authentic. The natural curve of her lower back and hips. Her slender arms and sleek neck, no scars from surgery to minimize Edward's Adam's. Susie's soft, round breasts aren't pumped up with silicone. And those powerful legs cradled by a thick and robust behind, and voluptuous hips — she would easily bear a child. A perfect cis woman. Childbearing hips. Cate couldn't match any of it.

"Yes, the painting is gorgeous. It looked great up at the cabin, too – that magical light!" Cate poked mischievously, masking her anger.

"Oh," Susie stumbled.

Cate knew she was uncomfortable. She enjoyed watching Susie squirm, caught off guard. Cate's claws were out and ready.

The tension in the room was thick. I need to get Susie out of here before chaos erupts. Hunter thought to himself.

Susie played with the pendant on her necklace, her fingers brushing her cleavage. "The cabins are a fun place to fish and swim, too. Hunter and I would fish off the banks for hours! Do you like to fish, Cate?" Susie flexed her own claws.

"No," Cate huffed.

"I suppose not. You don't look like the type," Susie scoffed.

Susie examined Cate from head to toe. Hunter saw her jealousy meet Cate's. He knew she saw how together Cate was — it was only early morning and she had on designer clothes, fresh makeup, and top of the line perfume. But she was also trying a little too hard. He knew the moment Susie realized the truth — Cate was like Hunter. She smirked as if she was superior. It was just like her. Cate was too caught up in battle to see his disdain, though. He had to end this confrontation.

"Susie, it was really nice to see you, but Cate and I have things to do." Hunter stated bluntly.

"I'm sorry I took up so much of your time." Susie stood up. "Hunter, don't you still have some of my belongings?"

Before Hunter could answer Cate went to the closet to retrieve her box. "Here you go! I hope you don't mind that I replaced everything. They don't match anymore." Cate spoke with contempt.

"You mean, like the make-up on your chest doesn't match your skin tone?" Susie shot back. Then she turned to Hunter. "If you change your mind about dinner, you know where to find the real deal." And just like that Susie floated away leaving only disorder and confusion.

"Bitch!" Cate said under her breath.

Hunter shut and locked the door behind Susie. "Well, that went well." Hunter laughed nervously.

"Really? I'm glad you think so." Cate went to bedroom and found her overnight bag.

"Every time things get tough… Is this really what you're going to do, leave?"

"You don't get it. How can I compete with her? Hunter, how? She is sophisticated, intelligent, beautiful, and she can have children. And she still wants you!" Cate folded her clothes, not looking up.

"Cate, I introduced you as my partner. She knows we're together." Hunter tugged at his beard.

"Well, I didn't see you stop her journey down memory lane. She practically undressed you with her eyes!"

"Cate, look at me! I'm right here. I have chosen you. There isn't any reason for your insecurity." Hunter picked up a towel from the kitchen and wiped the sweat off his face.

"Really? I remember a certain incident at a certain cabin that rocked my world and changed everything I knew about us! How do I know you're not lying now?" Cate started ripping and tearing the curtains away from the window. "These are mine, I guess. You probably will want to redecorate when she moves back in!"

Walking around the house she picked up any little item of sentimental value and jammed it in her overnight bag.

"What are you doing, Cate? This is ridiculous!" Hunter threw his hands up in the air.

"I will tell you what I'm afraid of. Giving my heart to you and you becoming reckless with it. Building a life together and in an instant having it shattered by a lie. Watching you around other woman and knowing that I'm just a duplication at best! That you can have any cis woman you want now – and that you'll leave me for her." Cate voice ruptured as she sat on the edge of the couch and cried silent tears.

"Whatever this is, whatever you're going through, I can't help you with that. Because I don't want Susie, or any cis woman. Only you can't see that! I love you, Cate but you're sabotaging this relationship."

"Can you promise you won't hurt me?" Cate turned to look at him.

"I can't promise you that. But I can promise it would never be intentional. All I can do is love you." Hunter wiped a tear away from her cheek.

"Well, our relationship is going to be tested." Cate interrupted.

"What do you mean?" Hunter responded.

Cate stood up and started picking up her mess. "I was going to tell you earlier, but things happened."

"Tell me what, Cate?" Hunter's tone became stern.

"I need to go away for a while. To treatment. I've been all right until now, but… it's still hard. I still want to use. I woke up wanting the pills. Maybe I even started this fight so I would have a reason to start using again. I'm a mess, Hunter." Cate took a sip of water. "But I'm going to treatment. I need to do this for me and do it right. I'm leaving as soon as a bed opens. I don't know what it'll mean for us. But if you could… watch over Smokey and my house? I could just leave my car here if you don't mind?"

"I'll take care of Smokey, and everything. But… when will you leave?" Hunter finally replied.

"In a week, maybe sooner. I'm clean, but the withdrawal is breaking me down. I sweat constantly and have a hard time concentrating."

Hunter held her shoulders. "What about work? How are you getting around that?"

"I have some vacation left and I'm going to take a leave of absence if I have to. I need to do this, Hunter. Can you..." Cate pleaded with her mystical eyes, casting a spell over Hunter that he welcomed.

"Cate, I want to help you I really do." Hunter stroked his face.

"Why do I feel there is a 'but' attached here?" Cate halted as her stomach flipped and turned with fear.

"Cate," Hunter looked deep in her eyes. "To be honest, it's hard for me to commit to you when you don't want to move in with me. What I'm saying is you need to figure us out. I feel you're asking me to do something that you would hesitate to do yourself."

Cate hung her head. "I don't want to move in, until I have handled this addiction. I want to be with you, Hunter, but this is what I need to do first. I love you. I do."

"Okay, okay, Cate. I love you too. We will get through this. Take it one day at a time."

Today was visiting day at the clinic. Hunter felt like a teenager getting ready for prom. A whole month had passed since he had spoken or seen Cate. Of course, they had been writing letters. The past month breathed new life into their relationship. Cate was beginning to open – delicately, gently. It was almost a spiritual experience to be witnessing her healing. Her confidence was growing as she learned through therapy why she always bottled her feelings up, and how fear of abandonment and addiction became ways to cope.

"I wish you could come today, Smokey. Your mom misses you something furious. We will get her home soon." Hunter picked up Smokey and kissed him lightly on his furry head. Hunter went to his closet to fetch a jacket. Cate should be out in the next couple weeks. He was going to stop by her house and pick up her mail, and make sure everything was all right.

Then he heard the car outside. Hunter looked out the window and saw a black coat but couldn't see a face. He was a little irritated when he opened the door; he didn't want to be late.

"Hello Hunter."

"Hi Susie.... I'm in a bit of a hurry." Hunter answered.

"This will only take a minute. Are you alone?" Susie grinned seductively. "I don't see another car. just your truck."

"Are you casing my house?" Hunter said sharply.

"I feel awful how things went down the last time I was here. Let me take you out to dinner. It will be like old times." Hunter caught a whiff of her perfume. It was one of the last gifts he bought her before their breakup.

"Can I use your restroom?" Susie requested pushing her way inside.

"Please hurry. I have an appointment!" Hunter closed the door hard, aggravated. He needed to get rid of Susie.

"Thanks, too many coffees. Where is your girlfriend? I mean is that what you call her?"

"Her name is Cate. What do you want Susie?" Hunter folded his arms.

"I told you." Susie moved close to him. "I want to talk. We could have dinner at my house if you would feel more comfortable. I could make my famous meatloaf and potatoes, your favorite, with a nice bottle of scotch afterward."

"Susie, I'm with someone. I'm leaving. Let's go!" Hunter escorted Susie to the front porch.

"I don't get it — what do you see in her? Lisa, she isn't a real woman like me!" Susie grabbed Hunter's arm.

"Don't call me Lisa. Obviously, you don't understand. Cate and I understand each other on a deeper level. I love her, Susie. That's all you need to know. She didn't walk out on me when things got tough. I'm leaving." Hunter brushed passed Susie and made his way to his truck.

"It must be hard going up to the cabin." Susie jerked around. "We have so much history there. Planting flowers, fishing, late nights by the open fire and well…. You know. Cate, is that her name? I'm sure her opinion of the cabin would change if she was aware that we had christened every room and a few places in the woods as well." Susie titled back against her car seductively.

Hunter slammed his truck door closed. "Susie, what do you want?"

"I want another chance. You owe me." Susie adjusted her blouse.

"How do I owe you?" Hunter was puzzled.

"For deceiving me so eloquently. I wanted to be with a woman and then without even really discussing it with me you proceeded with transitioning. Not even considering my feelings. My world was shattered! And I still miss you – you never gave me a chance to understand." Susie sat down on the porch.

"Are we going there again? I told you but you didn't want to listen. You didn't make things easy for me either. After that night you went on a rampage. Disappeared. You tore me down. I didn't know if you were cheating on me. I was just being honest with you and myself."

"That is just it, Hunter. It was always about you. Your friends, your house, your feelings. It was exhausting." Susie fretted.

"So, I'm confused. Susie, if I ruined your life and deceived you and exhausted you, why are you here?"

"The last time I saw you when you stopped by the house, I felt feelings I hadn't experienced since we broke up. I realized that it wasn't fair to resist you transitioning. Deep down, I always knew who you were and what you needed to do. The truth is I was just afraid. You know how biased and cruel our community can be. By you transitioning I would be known as that lesbian who is secretly a straight woman. We would be branded as selling out and becoming what we should despise, a heterosexual white couple. That's irrelevant now. I don't care what anyone thinks. Give me another chance. We have a history. Cate can't give you what I can." Susie moved toward Hunter, wrapped her sleek arms around his waist and laid her head on his gladiator chest.

An old familiar longing slowly crept up Hunter's spine making his hands tingle and stomach drop. He was aware it was just a physical reaction to Susie. She was so familiar. And Cate hadn't been available. He had missed her.

"Susie," Hunter gently removed her hands from his waist. "I never cared what other people thought about my choices. You did. I think you still do. What I did learn was that I needed to take myself through this journey. As far as Cate is concerned, she gives me what I need. You must figure this out – by yourself."

Hunter glanced in his rearview mirror. Susie was sloped on her car. He was glad he would see Cate today. They needed to connect. He couldn't go back to that old love with Susie. Cate has the key to my heart, he thought, and drove a little faster.

At the treatment center they searched him at the front door. Hunter figured they wanted to make sure you weren't smuggling any drugs or alcohol for their patients. Inside the corridor was a couch with some tables and chairs. People were visiting and drinking coffee. Some were laughing, others were silent, or crying. Hunter looked around for Cate and saw a flash of gold locks and heard an infectious laugh in a group of people at the window.

Cate was talking and laughing, and everyone was hanging onto her every word. Men surrounded her, and by the look in their eyes you could tell they were mesmerized by this exotic creature. Hunter was confused. Cate knew he was coming to see her, but she wasn't even looking for him, instead letting these men fall all over her.

Hunter stood for some time and watched Cate. She looked happy. She clearly didn't miss him at all. He walked over and stood beside her interrupting her conversation.

"Cate, can we talk somewhere private?" Hunter asked sternly.

"Hunter! Hi! How are you? Everyone, this is my friend, Hunter."

"Nice to meet you." A man said and extended his hand to Hunter.

Hunter declined to shake his hand. "Cate, can we leave now, please?"

Cate clicked her tongue, embarrassed by Hunter's rude behavior. "Hunter, what is wrong with you?"

"What is wrong with me? What is wrong with you? Falling all over those men and introducing me as your FRIEND! You knew that I was coming up today but instead I felt like I'm interrupting your party!" Hunter's voice was loud.

Cate's index finger touched her lips for Hunter to keep quiet. "Those men are my friends. They're in the program and have supported me this last month! I wanted you to meet them."

"Don't you have any female supporters? And do they know about the REAL you? Maybe they wouldn't be in such a hurry to get you into bed if they did!" Hunter raised his voice.

"You're being ridiculous!" Cate lashed back.

"Have you forgotten how I have been there for you? Taking care of house, car, Smokey, all your bills? I wanted to do it because we're together! I thought we were, anyway!" Hunter snapped.

Cate launched in closer "Stop making a scene. Wait what's that smell?" Cate sniffed his collar and neck. "Perfume! Why do you smell like perfume?" Cate was enraged. Her face flushed red. "Now I see. You're picking a fight to push me away."

"What…. What are you talking about?" Hunter tried to get his bearings.

"Who is she?" Cate interrogated.

"Oh. It's just — Susie stopped by before I came here." Hunter admitted.

Cate's mouth was wide open in disbelief. She sat down quickly her legs barely holding her up.

"Is this why you're attacking me? Because you're fucking her?" Cate pushed Hunter away.

"Don't push this back on me! Yes, she does want to get back together. I told her no, that it was too late, that I love you and we're moving on together. Because I thought we were." Hunter stated sharply.

"Really, how close to you was she with her cheap perfume? You haven't exactly been honest with me now have you, Hunter? First Stan. Now Susie." Cate turned away, suddenly sobbing.

"Are you OK, Cate?" A slender man came over, reaching out his hand.

"I'm OK, Frank, thank you." Cate reassured him.

"Hear that, Frank? She's OK!" Hunter puffed his chest out and stared angrily at Frank.

"Are you going to be rude to everyone? You don't know anything about these people. Frank just lost his wife to cancer. He's here dealing with alcoholism. Jim over there has chronic pain, and that's how he became an addict. They're my friends. They understand me. They've helped me! While you're out there exploring your options!"

"You know, Cate, I'm sorry to hear that about these people. But what about me? I have been out there keeping things in place until you could come home, while you're here playing therapist and flirting, and here I am, your FRIEND. Now I know why you didn't want to move in with me."

"Hunter, I love you, but I am working on me now. And you clearly are taking care of your own needs." Cate spoke softly, wiping away tears, suddenly calm.

The pain on Hunter's face was etched so deep that his face looked hard as stone. "So, you decided, I see. When were you going to tell me? Huh? In a letter. Maybe when I came to pick you up on graduation day. Better yet when you asked for Smokey back. You act like you love him, but you have not been there for him. I feed him; I take Smokey to his vet appointments. I'm there at night to greet him and love him. Well guess what. He is mine now!" Hunter pointed an accusing finger as Cate rose to her feet.

"Look Hunter, you're not hearing me. I'm not saying that I don't want to work it out. It's obvious we're in trouble. Getting clean cleared my head enough for me to realize that I need time. Please understand. If you don't want to watch my house or car, I get it, just give me some time to find someone else. I only have thirty days left. And no, you can't have Smokey." Cate added.

"I should have known this is what you do. Run when things get tough. I'm sure Gwen and Michael would agree with me!" Hunter's cheeks were fire engine red.

"I'm glad that I get to witness the real you before I agreed to move in with you. You can be cruel, Hunter, but you hid it well for a while."

"I gave you everything I had. My heart, time, support, and you're willing to throw it away, because you're confused. Welcome to the real world, Cate. Everyone gets confused. But I took a leap of faith for love. I guess it's not enough for you. I promised you that I would take care of your affairs while you were gone. That is what I will do. We will talk about the rest later." Hunter marched away in defeat.

"Cate, I'm sorry to interrupt, but the meeting is starting." Frank broke in.

"I'm coming, Frank. Hunter, I appreciate you taking care of Smokey and my personal affairs. Good luck with Susie, or whatever you want. I'm not going to let it stop me, no matter how much it hurts. I need time and you do too, apparently. I'll — call when I get home." Cate floated away gracefully.

Hunter had to fight off the urge to belt Frank in the eye when Cate took a seat near him. The man slanted in, solicitous; he had obviously saved that seat for her. Hunter balled his fists. He wanted to tear Frank apart from limb from limb but stormed out of the room.

On the drive home the hurt and rage were too much. Hunter pulled over. "Why?" Hunter screamed at the top of his lungs as he banged his hands on the steering wheel. The tears flowed rapidly down his face landing in his goatee and falling down his chest.

"I was there for her. I tried to show her what she means to me, but it didn't matter!" Hunter yelled out the window hoping someone would acknowledge his pain.

He turned the ignition on and began driving, letting the tears fall. He wanted to turn around and confront Cate, to explain, to make her love him again. When he barreled into his driveway, Smokey pushed open the drapes. At least there was someone waiting for him. He needed to cuddle with Smokey. He rested his head on the window to gather himself before going inside.

CHAPTER 15

"Hunter, are you OK?"

A familiar voice disturbed him from a deep sleep. He was still in his truck, disoriented. "Susie, what do you want?" Hunter said gruffly.

"I lost my wallet. I have looked everywhere. Maybe it's inside. I know you said not to come back, so can you check for me? It's pink. You can't miss it. I will wait here." Susie stepped back from his truck.

Hunter opened his door and tried to hide his red eyes from Susie. "You can come in and look."

Susie smiled and followed him inside.

"I need to use the restroom. Then I'll have a look." Hunter shut the bathroom door and splashed his face with cold water. He was feeling sick to his stomach and realized it was time for his T shot. He unbuckled his jeans and sat down on the toilet drawing the magical fluid into the syringe. The popping noise was familiar and sent a wave of calmness and normalcy throughout his body. He splashed some more water on his face before turning the doorknob to go out.

"I found it." Susie exclaimed. "Thanks." Susie motioned toward the front door, her skirt hiked up just enough that Hunter caught a glimpse of her fishnet stockings and sexy thighs.

What the hell, he thought to himself. "Wait! Have a drink with me."

Hunter was aware of the risk involved with Susie staying but at this point he didn't care. The black hole in his chest was a gaping wound and he was desperate to fill it by whatever means necessary.

"I would love to." Susie sat down with her dancer legs crossed at her feet.

"So, what is going on with you these days?" Hunter said as he poured the scotch.

"Hunter, you look upset?" Susie took a long sip. "Where's your lady friend?

"What? I can't ask you how you have been?"

"Where is she? Cate, is it?"

"She isn't here."

"I can see that. Did you break up?" The inflection in her voice was cheerful.

"I'm not sure what's going on, to be honest. Probably." Hunter gulps his drink and pours another.

"Talk to me." Susie turned her body inward touching Hunter's leg.

Hunter didn't want to talk about Cate, but he needed to get a few things off his chest. "She had to leave town for a while and I'm taking care of her house and, Smokey of course." Smokey settled on the rug by his feet. "I don't know what's going on with her. She has men falling all over her and she is very vague about how she feels about our relationship. Whatever. I don't know."

Susie poured Hunter another drink, and then another. Soon the bottle was empty, and the old familiar jokes started, and their comfortable drunken routine settled in. Hunter talked and she commiserated. Soon they were cuddling close.

"Well, I'm a woman and I know first-hand if she is giving you the cold shoulder and the "I need to figure things out" speech, she is interested in someone else. I hate to tell you that, but I think you already know it." Susie suggested with a hint of satisfaction like a cat who finally catches the mouse.

Hunter held up the bottle. "I should have some water…" He moved to stand up, but Susie stopped him.

"Hunter I'm sorry that I wasn't there for you. I was being selfish. I thought it was Lisa I fell in love with, and I couldn't see past that. But I was wrong. It was you. Always." Susie touched Hunter's face and patted his hair.

The softness of a woman's hand was soothing, and Hunter was drunk. He missed Cate, too. He closed his eyes. His mind wandered back to the cabin, the fire crackling in the fireplace, the fresh potato soup simmering on the stove. Cate's lips pulling him into her, and him, wanting to ravish her then and there. His head was swimming in ecstasy. He could sense her heat and breath on his mouth.

Susie was like a tourist enjoying the sites. She ran her fingertips slowly around the collar of his shirt. Her hands found their way to his defined chest and gently pulled out his shirt tail and traced the rough bumps that were once Lisa's breasts. She began to explore his groin, curious about the changes there.

Hunter let out a slight moan. Colors and patterns swirled in his head. Between the rising heat in his groin and Susie's warm hands on his chest, he was about to erupt. The clanking of metal on his belt and his zipper startled him out of his lustful stupor.

"Susie!" Hunter opened his eyes to her victorious grin. He was wide awake now and redoing his belt buckle. "I'm sorry, I can't! I mean, you smell wonderful and are soft and so like I remember. But I won't do this."

Susie remained on his lap. "You had no problems a few minutes ago." Susie's eyes darted to Hunter's rising package. "Listen I want this. I want to see what's new! I won't tell Cate. Hunter, this is between us." Susie bent down and kissed his neck, knowing from experience it was a turn-on.

"Susie!" Hunter grabbed her hands. "I'm in love with her. Even if she doesn't – I still love her."

Hunter could see the shock written all over her face. "Where does that leave me, Hunter? That girl who you experimented with and messed with and left behind? First, we're together for years as lesbians, and then you decided you want to become a man. Then you come flaunt your transition in front of me. And now you ask me to stay have a drink with you, leading me on just to shut me down!" Susie jumped off his lap.

"What! That's not it at all!" Hunter felt more and more sober. "I just wasn't thinking, Susie. I was upset. Even if Cate decides she won't have me back, I can't cheat on her, not now. I love her! And she – Susie, all those years together, you never got it. We were together when I had my chest surgery and I told you many times about how this transition would go. You saw the pamphlets from my doctor office. I didn't leave you in the dark! You didn't want to listen. I don't think you really want me, not now. Not like you think." Hunter stood up and put some distance between them, opening a can for Smokey who was scolding him for being late with his dinner.

"You selfish bastard!" Susie launched her heel at Hunter's head.

Hunter ducked just in time. Smokey flew out of the kitchen and flew underneath the couch.

"Oh, shit Susie!" Hunter picked up his uncle's painting. "There is a hole in it!" Hunter tried to contain his anger. "This is the only painting I have from him."

"Oh, so what, Hunter!" Susie fetched her heel and tried to put it on. "Dammit. I need to leave."

"No, you're not going anywhere drunk. You can have my bed. I will sleep on the couch." Hunter locked the front door and went to the closet to retrieve a pillow and blanket. He sat on the couch touching the edge of the gaping hole in the painting.

"Hunter." Susie walked toward him. "I'm really sorry."

"Just go to sleep." Hunter laid down and turned away. "Smokey, come on boy!"

Hunter pretended to be asleep until he heard the bedroom door close. Smokey's constant purring finally lulled him to sleep.

The next morning Hunter woke to a throbbing head and a pulse beating through his ears. Smokey was twisted up in a ball by his feet. The birds chirping out the window didn't help with his hangover.

I need some water, Hunter thought to himself. The floor felt good, cold on his bare feet. His throat was tight and dry, and he drank the water fast. His head started spinning.

He made his way towards the bedroom. The door was open, and the bed made. Susie had left a note.

Hunter,
I'm sorry about your painting. Please forgive me. I hope you find what you're looking for. Take care.
Susie.

Hunter sat on the edge of the bed and reached for the aspirin on the nightstand. He needed to get away. He wanted to clear his head. He had to come up with some new ideas to write about, a new book to pitch to his agent. Maybe Robert wants to go fishing at the cabin, he thought to himself. He nuzzled the cat's neck. "It's time to focus on me, Smokey."

Over the next week, Hunter outlined a new novel. He started walking around his neighborhood again and enjoying spring in its full bloom. He made sure Cate's yard and house looked good and started packing for his fishing trip to the cabin. He might stay for a while. Robert would come for a few days, too.

Smokey paced all over his clothes, butting the duffel bag he was packing. "Don't worry buddy, you're coming with me this time."

Hunter couldn't stop thinking about Cate. She would be home in a few weeks, and he wanted to have Smokey a little longer before she eventually came to pick him up.

Hunter had accepted that Cate was pulling away. Her letters had changed since their fight. They were shorter, focused less on their future and more on her recovery and her new friends. She worried about finding the right sponsor. It was clear their relationship wasn't her priority.

He felt resentful and hurt, but he kept his letters matter of fact. He talked about his day-to-day activities and not his feelings. The wall was high.

"Let's have a vacation, before I have to miss you!" Hunter said to Smokey as he tried to entice him inside the cat carrier. Hunter's eyes were teary. It would be hard to lose Smokey.

Smokey squawked the whole car ride. Hunter laughed and felt himself relax. The colors coming back to life against the mountain were exactly what his tired soul needed. Disappearing to the crystal-clear blue lakes would be a welcome break from the city and Hunter's aching heart.

Hunter came to a stop at the cabin, and when the dust settled, he saw Robert's bright yellow truck and his German Shephard, Bo. "Hey there, about time! You were always late." Robert jibed.

"You can't rush perfection. Will Smokey be OK with Bo?" Hunter asked.

"I would worry about Bo more than Smokey. They'll be fine – Bo's a sweetheart. Let's unpack. I want to fish!"

They spent the rest of the day fishing while Smokey explored the cabin and Bo ran down by the lake.

"I love the air down here by the lake. It ripples on the water." Robert observed. "Want a beer?" Hunter nodded and caught a cold one. "Speaking of beautiful, where is Cate?"

"We had a fight. She needed some space. In other words, she is seeing someone else." Hunter cast his line into the calm water.

"Do you really believe that or are you giving up?" Robert challenged Hunter.

"What is that supposed to mean?" Hunter grunted.

"It means that after all this time you are still holding on to what Stan did to you. You give up on love, you let him win. Stop carrying around that bullshit. Cut it the fuck loose, man."

"What does that have to do with Cate?" Hunter found a stick to prop up his fishing pole.

Robert gulped the last drop of beer and crushed the can like a caveman. "Are you kidding me? She's probably seeing other people. You don't know, do you. You didn't really ask! You're frozen in time, Hunter. I'm no therapist but what I do see is Lisa trying to figure out if she is worthy of love, and Hunter giving up on a good thing. The way I see it, you and Cate belong together. Don't let this one go." Robert slapped Hunter on his back.

Hunter was amazed. Was he giving up because of some warped self-fulfilling prophecy? That was Cate's crap, not his. But he had a funny feeling. Maybe he had just assumed they were over.

At sunset they retrieved their catch for the day and headed back for dinner.

"I will clean the fish. Why don't you go down and check out where you want to plant the flowers tomorrow," Robert suggested.

"Good idea." Hunter lit a cigarette and walked down to planting area. He squatted in front of the rich, weedy earth, and soaked up the beauty around him.

"Dad, I miss you. I wish you were here to guide me. Cate has my heart, and I don't know where we're going. Remember how much you wanted a birdfeeder by the sunflowers? Well, after I plant the flowers. I'm going to build one right by the oak tree. There are signs of you everywhere. The Cardinal couple comes back to same tree. The dragonflies are everywhere this year. I'm thinking about moving here, maybe next year, fulltime. Would you like that? Anyway, thank you for believing in me, I love you." Hunter touched the earth that cradled his father's ashes.

Back at the cabin Robert and Hunter ate dinner while Bo played with Smokey, who finally cuddled into the dog bed with his new buddy. After a few beers, Hunter and Smokey went into the bedroom. Images filled his mind of loving Cate here, in this room. The bed was full of her. Remembering her body, her moans, her long eyelashes brushing against his lips sending jolts of electricity throughout his body. His body ached remembering being inside her.

Smokey could sense his restlessness and bumped his face. "Try to get some sleep boy. You're coming with me early to the garden tomorrow."

The next day Hunter gathered some tools and water to take down with him to the field. Robert was going into town with Bo for supplies. Smokey was chasing butterflies and grasshoppers as they walked down to the garden showing off his jumping ability. He never strayed too far from his side, which Hunter was grateful for. Out in the wilderness he could run into danger. Hunter kept his eye on the playful cat. The high noon heat was breaking through and Hunter sat on a tree stump with Smokey at his feet for a much-needed water break.

"Here you go boy." Hunter cupped his hand for Smokey to lap water from.

"I thought I would find you here."

Hunter looked over his shoulder. "Cate!" Hunter splashed his shoe with Smokey's water.

"Smokey! I missed you!" Cate reached down to greet Smokey, who ran to her side. Hunter thought she looked wonderful. He cleared his throat.

Cate picked Smokey up. How could she tell Hunter how she really felt after their fight at the meeting, after all those cold letters? The truth was she loved him, but she didn't know how to let anyone love her. She knew that, but could Hunter accept it? That it would take some time? That she wanted to try?

"Hunter," Cate sat down by the tree stump and let Smokey plop in her lap. She felt nervous and was glad for Smokey's comfort. "Just listen. I know I treated you poorly these last couple months. I had to focus on my recovery. For the first time in a long time, I had to face up to my own – to myself. I didn't know how to talk about us. Everything seemed different. But one thing that hasn't changed is how I feel about you. I love you. Please forgive me?"

Hunter took a deep breath. "I was hurt. I'm not going to lie. But I know you needed to work on yourself. I can come on strong but it's because I know what I want. I still want you. There was nothing with Susie, Cate. But I'm not going to chase you. You need to decide."

"I thought that I made my decision clear by coming here." Cate reached for his hand. "So…. Where do we go from here?" Cate asked.

"Well, you could help me plant these flowers." Hunter smiled.

"Only if you share your dad's tools. You get possessive of his stuff. I will not ruin this beautiful manicure digging with my hands."

"It looks like we both have our work cut out for us." Hunter handed Cate the spade.

"Yes. But I wouldn't want to be anywhere else." Cate gently touched Hunter's face.

"Me either, Cate. Me either."

THE END

ACKNOWLEDGEMENTS

I want to thank my creative team, Carol, Rachel, and Patrise.
My vision was cultivated gently with your hands.

To my family and friends your unwavering support
brought me to the finish line.

ABOUT THE AUTHOR

Val Gale was born and raised in Des Moines, Iowa. He served in The US Army from1991 to 1996, stationed in New York and Seoul, Korea. He completed a B.A. in 1999 from Grandview University in Des Moines after his honorable discharge. He identifies as trans.

He focuses full time on his writing since an industrial accident amputated his hand and ended his work in a tire facility, creating an opportunity to pursue his lifelong passion for creative fiction. His first novel, *Different*, a semi-autobiographical YA novel about a trans teen, was published in 2017. He recently completed *Hunter*, an LGBTQ novel telling the story of post-transition trans relationships.

He is currently working on an LGBTQ suspense novel and experimenting with short fiction.